WHAT BOOKS PRESS

AN IMPRINT OF

THE GLASS TABLE

COLLECTIVE

LOS ANGELES

RHOMBUS
AND OVAL

JESSICA SEQUEIRA

WHAT
BOOKS
PRESS

LOS ANGELES

'A journey that leaves no trace', 'Animal spirits', 'A useless object', 'Conversation outside El Pastizal', 'Bar Británico', 'Golden triangle' and 'Transformation' were published by *Berfrois*. 'Inflamed eye' was published by *Glasgow Review of Books*. 'Anatomy of a hold-up', 'Back of the head', 'La Invisibla' and 'Perfection' were published by *Queen Mob's Teahouse*. 'Enchanted boat' and 'Perrine' were published by *Entropy*. 'In the rose garden' was published by *Sounds and Colours*.

Publisher's Cataloging-In-Publication Data

Names: Sequeira, Jessica.
Title: Rhombus and oval / Jessica Sequeira.
Description: Los Angeles : What Books Press, [2017] | Some of the stories in this book were published previously by Berfrois, Entropy, Glasgow Review of Books, Queen Mob's Teahouse and Sounds and Colours.
Identifiers: ISBN 978-0-9962276-7-4
Subjects: LCSH: United States--Fiction. | Argentina--Fiction. | LCGFT: Short stories.
Classification: LCC PS3619.E68 R46 2017 | DDC 813/.6--dc23

Cover art: Gronk, *untitled*, mixed media on paper, 2016
Book design by Ash Good, www.ashgood.design

What Books Press
363 South Topanga Canyon Boulevard
Topanga, CA 90290

WHATBOOKSPRESS.COM

RHOMBUS
AND OVAL

CONTENTS

*What would it matter, what would it change
if these pages were written in Buenos Aires?*

RHOMBUS AND OVAL

THE FIRST SHAPE to cross the sky was a rhombus, green with a solid black outline. It didn't move quickly, but its maneuvers were performed with a certain élan. When it arrived at its intended destination, it paused as if to gauge its next step; then it continued to another place and disappeared from view. My first reaction was to doubt my eyes. My vision isn't good, and what's more I understand it's incredible to claim I saw a geometric form above the city, ordinary as a cloud or airplane. But I remained quiet; I dislike calling attention to myself. In the end, what difference does a rhombus make?

The next morning a beautiful oval joined the rhombus. Blue and bordered by delicate gold dashes, it moved with great lightness. At first I mistook it for a kite. I thought of remaining quiet, but this seemed to cross some inexplicable limit. Besides, I was curious if I was the only one to perceive such forms. 'Have you seen . . . ?' I asked the doorman of my apartment, lifting my eyes toward the sky. He examined me warily, then relaxed. 'It's good you see them too,' he said. 'Or else I'd have begun to doubt.' Since he is the down-to-earth type, I trusted him. But now that the sighting was confirmed, what could we do?

My doorman looked from his post at the crowd passing. I've always admired the way he keeps so still amidst the people rushing everywhere. 'We should take them down to examine them more carefully,' he said. 'If they're beautiful we can recreate them, if dangerous destroy them. In either case we'll be acting in the public interest.' My first reaction was that the idea was mad, but first reactions are often knee-jerk and misguided. I waited for it to dissolve so a second and more interesting idea could emerge. Perhaps he was right, after all. Why not? Life is occasionally very beautiful and occasionally very hostile, but more often than not it is very strange. Frequently you must let yourself be carried along by the current, counter to the smooth dictates of logic.

'How should we go about it?' I asked. 'Ladder?,' he proposed with a thoughtful look. Then he shook his head. 'No, airplane. Or helicopter.' I voiced the concern that we didn't own one. This was immediately brushed aside. 'A friend who owes me a favor will let us borrow his,' he said. After that I had no more objections.

The house of the friend was not the *chalet* I expected from someone with a helicopter, but a modest residence with a front garden. The man who opened seemed sympathetic, and when he'd heard us out he nodded. 'To tell the truth I hadn't noticed anything up there, but I admit I'm somewhat of a recluse. Since my wife's death . . . but no one wants to hear other people's sentimental stories. Let's go.' We went to the helicopter, and all at once were in the sky. It was beautiful to look out the window at the pure blue, passing through the inside of a cloud to move into pure blue once more.

The journey was not free of doubts. At one point the rhombus even disappeared completely. Had we calculated incorrectly and lost it, or were we now inside it? What would we do with it once we got a hold of it? We didn't even have a precise idea of its size. It might be much larger or much tinier than we'd imagined when we had viewed it from Earth. I began to communicate these new considerations, but all at once the doorman held a finger to his lips. There the two shapes were, floating, shining before us.

After carefully looping a steel wire around them and drawing them to the helicopter, we descended, then unloaded them at the doorman's house in the provinces. They were kept in the backyard with the rabbits, first as a secret and then openly. The shapes behaved well, making no noise and doing nothing out of the ordinary. 'At least they don't eat anything,' said the doorman's mother, looking at them out of the corner of her eye. Still unsure of their preferences, I took them with me on short excursions, guiding them on a leash to school, library, supermarket.

The rhombus seemed to enjoy being admired. With praise it grew tense and vibrated, assuming a charming tone slightly more violet than usual. The oval, in contrast, went pale in the presence of other beings, preferring to remain at home. These initial, subtle distinctions soon deepened into more marked differences. The rhombus appealed to those with restless and roving spirits, while the oval made itself visible to more quiet domestic types. The rhombus picked up the trick of mirroring the color of its surroundings and could soon flash a number of gaudy colors in rapid succession, while the oval glowed a steady milky white.

It became clear, too, that most people were capable only of perceiving one or the other, not both. Perhaps this is not so strange in itself. Many phenomena we think of as enigmatic would be natural were we to possess more senses. Five is an arbitrary number, based on perceptions of a specific space and time. Often a perception offers a faint illumination, suggesting another possible sense linked to no organ we know. And if we already have senses we don't fully understand, perhaps we might also develop new senses, capable of perceiving the mysterious . . .

I have time to think about big things like this anyhow, since the rhombus and oval are no longer with me. It's not just me that will miss them. My doorman surprised me with his concern for their well-being and constant search for little gifts to make them happy. His mother came to love them too, asking whether this or that behavior on their part was normal, and helping them into the new scarves and collars her son bought, adapted to their individual tastes.

But at some point all of us could see clearly that both shapes were growing restless. The rhombus increasingly strained at its leash, and I knew it wanted to see the world. The oval, for all it liked to stay at home, began to elongate itself at night in its cage, stretching its elliptical shadow into the courtyard to better see its beloved sky and stars. 'Homesick' was the matter-of-fact diagnosis of the porter's mother, and I knew she was right.

With a combination of pride and resignation to the inevitable, we decided to let the two of them go. The rhombus remained on earth, but since it has its own career now and is always traveling, I hardly ever see it. The oval was released into the sky, where it shows itself with relative frequency. Knowing it will appear helps me to remain calm, and few things make me happier than those clear hours of afternoon and night when it can be seen above. Look up— there it is even now, right there.

A JOURNEY THAT LEAVES NO TRACE

I USED TO WORK at a translation agency, where two large windows looked out onto the city. From one you could see Retiro station, where a train deposited us every morning after gathering us up from the provinces. That was the view from the room where the secretaries sat, answering the telephone with smooth practiced voices. Occasionally they got up to make coffee, adding milk heated and foamed just so, and delivered it to the bosses in their private offices.

The other window was in the room with the translators. Our view was of a giant billboard with a perfume advertisement. The figures in it moved, assuming different positions each day, even changing clothing. When I first saw this happening, I thought I was just tired after a long day of staring at the screen. Strange things happen when you look at a computer for too long. Your head swims, small floating dots appear, an afterglow remains even after you've shut the apparatus and gone home. But someone reassured me that a system of sensors really was making the figures move.

During the day I hardly ever left the office. There was no need to: the company provided us with coffee, tea, light snacks (rice cakes and instant soup), a substantial lunch. The faint, pleasant scent of some fresh flower wafted through the air, never overpowering.

In my dreams I visited the other levels. Floor 27 was like being in a satellite. The night I went there I watched a movie about a couple of Los Angeles hackers who initiated communication with US space contractors from their garage. They painted a window on the wall to make it look like they were speaking from an office. Security breaches had been detected, they said. All they requested in exchange for sealing leaks was employment; the capitalist dream remained intact.

Floor 3 was a wooded grove. Floor 14 was completely underwater. If you didn't like what was happening you could always get back in the elevator and go to a different level. The elevator only jammed once, sealing me in its metal walls with just a single other person for company.

*

When it was announced that by official order all the world's texts would be digitized, and that all new written content must be uploaded online, some people were upset. Certain left-wing magazines presented their counterpoints in strongly worded editorials: a lack of privacy, a further consolidation of power of the company already controlling the government, etc. Other publications expressed cautious support, but remained skeptical it could be done. In the end, none of these articles mattered. The project would move ahead regardless.

As for me, I had no firm opinions. I'd just been let go from another company and was thinking pragmatically. The new law opened up hundreds of jobs, including my current position at the Data Office. I'm hardly a political romantic, or any kind of romantic at all (or so I thought then). At first I felt empty, like I was simply doing one thing after another without meaning. It was a certain strangeness I assumed would pass. Then like everyone else I got used to it.

'Home', the place I went when the day ended, was a room shared with two other girls always sleeping when I arrived. They spent almost their entire day in bed. At first I thought they went to sleep early because they were early risers, but when I left the house they were still there: two lumps occasionally rustling gently, finding warm refuge and peace in some world other than this rubble-filled corner in the south of the city. A camera eye followed me as

I left the house. I imagined the landlord sitting in his residence two blocks away, revising the footage. I didn't waste much time in my own place. The anonymity of the office was preferable, where although I knew I was being watched just as closely, it at least seemed impersonal. The personal had begun to seem something sinister.

*

At the office my language pair was French and English, which may not seem intuitive for someone in a Spanish speaking country. But now that everything is virtual and invisibly connected, physical location matters little. 'Translation' was a loose term for what we did there anyway. It would be more accurate to say monitoring, or revising. The mandate from above was clear: everything must have an English copy. The computer produced a rough version, which we edited; it didn't have to be 'literary', but did have to read cleanly.

Most of the texts that came my way were legal or business-related. As I worked I felt myself becoming a machine, efficient at replacing phrases with their equivalents, rearranging where necessary, using the translation software installed on all computers in an economic but judicious way. The texts were delivered via a kind of inbox with just one button, 'reply'. The only recipient was the company, which managed further delivery of texts to third parties and firms. Payment was the fifth of each month, through direct deposit to our bank accounts.

Only very rarely did a different kind of text come my way, one not merely informative like the others. Those were the materials that gave me the most pleasure. A new series began to arrive in my inbox one day, from a professor at a small US university writing a book on Céline. He needed all the author's personal letters translated fast, in order to fulfill the terms of a book deal previously negotiated with an academic publisher.

These details about the requester never came to me officially, of course. The idea, as with the one-button inbox, was to preserve anonymity. But gossip still hadn't been completely eradicated. I'm not sure how widespread what we did was, how porous the exchange of information. There were hundreds of these offices all over the world. If I weren't afraid of being paranoid, I might even say the company encouraged it, to maintain translators' interest in their work. Apathy was just as detrimental to final product quality as excess of interest, as careful studies paid for by the company demonstrated.

*

It was my colleague Luis who told me about the professor. Something had happened between Luis and me a few days before after the end-of-year party, and we were still nervous around each other. He was a database programmer, and that night he explained his work to me in general terms: how the idea of 'disappearing' is increasingly antiquated, something ever more difficult to achieve given today's modern informational networks; how ultra-modern computers can piece together anyone's motives by connecting isolated phrases and offhand remarks across distinct social networks and data platforms, tracing them geographically; how a second-order contextual narrative of meaning is constructed.

While he teased out the implications, I finished off several glasses of champagne. Soon I was giggling and clinging to his arm as he threaded us through the crowd in the main office to his private workspace, in one of the rooms without windows. There he pulled up the database with unconcealed pride.

'Give me a name. Not someone famous, that's no fun. Someone who isn't too documented. An X.'

I named the professor.

'Single middle-aged male with a colorful past. Expatriate abroad in Paris for several years, where he lived *à la bohème* and fell in love with the French avant-garde novelists and poets. Now languishing at a backwater US university with a literature department under strain. Classes consistently register low or even, once, no enrollment. Professional existence constantly self-questioned. He himself has lost faith in his books. Removed from their environment they become dead texts, just as absurd to him as his students. Calls to revolution shouted into a cornfield. In addition he perceives a certain contradiction in making them his subjects. Tying them up in neat packages, exposing them to analyses they themselves would reject. Isn't it more interesting to keep things obscure? Isn't that what attracted him to them in the first place? Some depth not quite penetrable, some siren call to a romantic utopia beyond the bounds of department-funded rational comprehension? He's farmed out these translations, and the university, far from scandalized, praises his efficiency. If all goes well, come September he'll be lying in a hammock in Maui, with a tropical cocktail in hand and a great angst.'

Luis rattled all this off imperturbably, his report peppered with phrases taken directly from the professor's online correspondence. As I listened, I put my hand on his shoulder, the words filling me with both awe and an indefinable fear.

*

I was glad I knew the professor's story, which I kept in mind as I worked. At night I'd begun reading Céline's work, underlining phrases: 'tous ces pays-là qui brûlaient, devant soi et des deux côtés, avec des flammes qui montaient et léchaient les nuages.' I had come to the language through literature, not the avant-garde but those writers who saw clearly how human beings are, Balzac and Stendhal and Flaubert and Zola.

Reading Céline made me feel strange, dizzy. The dots leading precisely nowhere, the idea of an unredeemable mankind, the rhythm and slang of vulgar speech, death on the installment plan, disdain, fascistic touches, invective . . . even though I read all his books on a screen, unlike the Balzac paperbacks I lovingly caressed as a teenager, they still filled me with a strange energy bordering on fury. It was impossible to read just a few pages then sleep. Luis and I kept discussing the professor during breaks. Updates on his mood and movements, tracked through the database, were an excellent way to pass the time, and avoid talking about us. Luis told me the professor would soon be going to California to research the life of a ballerina, the woman Céline was obsessed (or in love?) with. Hearing the professor would be traveling gave me the idea.

I would find him and meet him in person; he'd become more than just a series of data fragments. By this point Céline has been consecrated by the academy, and his life journey is well-marked out for the tourist. But that's just what attracted me to the professor. He was malleable and living; the vital current still flowed electric. Perhaps I could even intervene in his life or his book. I didn't know how just yet, but it didn't matter. I was tired of being a medium, of having words pass through me. Now I wanted to create.

That morning I stupidly told Luis what I was thinking, even asked him to accompany me. He looked at me without responding, not understanding. If I were to explain things well, I know he'd want to go; but I also knew he'd be too weak to ever actually leave. A contempt grew within me, perhaps a distorted form of the desire to really live.

When my day at the office finished, I came to a lackluster bar, where at one of the tables I worked out my plan. Piles of notes lay stacked up around me: Céline's novels, critical commentaries, biographies, maps of the western United States.

*

In the dream I'm dreaming now, which so far as I know no computer is registering, an airplane takes me from Ezeiza to LAX. Outside my window, the sky extends outward without limit. I lose myself in the transparent air, dissolve in the blue.

When I arrive at the professor's house, there's no answer. I call the university, whose representatives are just as much in the dark as I am. Where has he gone? The door before me is mute. I decide to enter. The knob turns without resistance. In the first room in which I set foot, there is a computer, turned on and open to the professor's sent mail. Unable to help myself, I read what is written. At first it confuses me, then I understand. It is a love letter.

> *What would I do if you were to leave this earth now? Remain quiet, likely. Join in the general mourning without drawing special attention to the nature of our friendship. At best they'd ask (if you, or I, were a little more famous) for a contribution to some volume, a tribute made not at the end of someone's long and distinguished career in the German way, but posthumously. I would watch as your husband spoke, your family and friends.*

I am connected to none of it, and even those that recognize my face wouldn't think of asking me to speak about you. Perhaps they'd suspect some strange currents passed darkly under the surface, but consider it wiser to maintain the tranquility of things. Let sleeping secrets lie, stir no stick to muddy the waters.

Or perhaps they would have no idea of our past. Even I have my doubts at times. Viewed in retrospect, the shivering barely-there threads of imagined association, certain lines in emails and letters corresponding with one another beyond what is written, might evaporate, appear mere paranoia. Were they to vanish, giving way to the dominant narrative of your life, I would be negated absolutely.

Lola, I'm coming. While you're still here I need to know if you care for me. If you ever did.

I stand holding the letter in my hand for a minute. Then I reach into my pocket, pull out my lighter and return ticket, and flick the metal circle. The flames are gorgeous. The grand country is waiting. The doors of the elevator spring open to take me there.

CONVERSATION OUTSIDE EL PASTIZAL

IN THE STREET in front one day, a man I'd just been introduced to began to tell a story. He'd been crossing Corrientes and Uruguay on a red when a motorbike passing between cars, in a maneuver as illegal as his own, collided with him. The *moto* sped off without stopping; as the man continued to lie there, sprawled face down on the ground, a crowd circled. When he opened his eyes, a homeless man with dirty face was leaning over him, waving a hand over his leg.

'Go away, I'm okay,' said the man, irritated. 'I'm going to cure you,' said the vagabond. 'No need, I'm okay,' repeated the man. He felt the warm hands of the vagabond and tried to kick him off. 'Hey you, I said I'm alright, are you deaf?' 'He says he's alright, I cured him!' the vagabond cried with joy, addressing himself to the crowd. Just then a policeman pushed through and noticed the scene. 'Get moving now, come along,' said the cop to the vagabond, giving him a shove. More police began to arrive and break up the crowd; the vagabond dropped from sight, disappearing down an obscure side street. 'Now he's probably bragging to everyone about his achievement,' said the man to us, his half-attentive listeners, while laughing and rubbing his knee.

The bell rang and the others went in for drinks, the anecdote already forgotten; I decided to stay a while longer in the fresh air. We were in a *barrio* a bit far from the center, where the street was quiet and cars rarely passed. The man who had spoken remained outside too, but now his performer's face looked serious and tired. 'Were you able to catch anything in what I said?' he asked suddenly. 'Sometimes I think no one understands when I try to explain. Every real event has a phantom explanation—'

'I think so,' I said. 'Something similar happened to me. Last year I left a notebook at Bar Lavalle and when I realized, I sent an email asking the owner whether it'd been found. The answer came back negative, and I never did recover it—by the way, if anyone you know finds a pale pink notebook with black cursive writing and notes on a book called *El nervio óptico* as well as more personal subjects, I'd appreciate if he or she could contact me. It must be around somewhere, things don't usually just disappear. Anyway, ever since then the restaurant has sent weekly emails with a copy of its menu, headed by a literary quote. I'm fond of them, though I'm aware of how saccharine they are.'

'This morning the line was from Giacomo Leopardi's *El infinito*—"And into this immensity my thought sinks ever drowning / and it is sweet to shipwreck in such a sea". Below was the menu, aubergine milanesas gratinadas with squash purée, fillets al champiñón with Noisette potatoes, fresh salmon accompanied by vegetable wok, palm heart and kani kama salad. I found the words beautiful, and so I copied down this meaningless list. But it occurred to me that were I to stop and attempt to communicate my reasons for creating such a catalogue, the reasoning would have to proceed as follows.'

'Nothing exists beyond close noticing. No idea goes beyond pure observation. Description alone, not narrative or philosophy, gives reading pleasure. Atmospheric instability requires the quick capture of moments. Only instantaneous description ensures comprehension. The historian follows a few steps behind, working from the burnt fragments of shells long detonated. I thought this, yet I couldn't bring myself to believe it. Isn't there something that goes beyond lists? Isn't there a significance beyond the surface layer of events? Isn't there—'

'I see you understand,' the man interrupted. 'Now I can trust you with a full explanation. Art may be what gives beauty and meaning to life, but a living doesn't earn itself. Until yesterday my job was to stand outside restaurants and entice people in by distributing flyers. Most were ignored or looked at briefly then tossed in the street. It didn't matter. Even if no one entered I was paid the same. So I tried to get rid of promo materials as fast as possible. Repetition brought comfort with this mechanical execution, this identical gesture performed again and again. Walking up and down the same street hundreds of times created a routine. I passed the same people—an old professor who drank coffee outside a café at a certain hour, old friends now housewives who do their shopping in the neighborhood. The same shops and statues too, and the same personal landmarks like a certain hotel.'

'A hotel—what's so interesting about that, you might ask? But this one had something special about it. Viewed from different angles, it seemed to possess either one, two or three chimneys. It wasn't something I noticed at first. Passing so often and at different times of day, though, the true number began to obsess me. A gap between two apartment buildings formed a passageway; I could settle my doubt once and for all. During my afternoon shift, unable to control myself, I began to make my way down the path. As I continued it seemed to grow increasingly narrow, the air increasingly thin. At some point I even found it difficult to walk. But at last I reached the end.'

'When I arrived at the boundary and looked up, there it was. It rose up so suddenly it was impossible to make out the number of chimneys, or even the building's true height. The way it leaned forward posed a threat. Something beyond your grasp will always exist, it suggested. Something you can't fathom. A second or third or even fourth chimney. A flickering presence, inexplicable, beyond the known. Ah! I grew so frightened I turned around and retraced my steps. All I wanted was to never return, never set eyes on that building again. In my hurry to get away I crossed the street without looking. There was a buzz in my head, everything began to shimmer. That was when the motorbike—'

The bell rang a second time. Neither of us wanted to miss the performance, so we went in search of those we'd arrived with. The conversation came abruptly to an end. It was a relief to watch the *sainete*, the one-act comedy that followed, pleasantly clear in its absence of phantom interpretations. After the show I went on to a pizzeria; the man made no further appearance.

A few days later, sitting in a café in the center, I read an opinion piece in *La Nación* related to current elections. The previous night four presidential speeches had been streamed live on television from the Patio de las Palmeras at the Casa Rosada, before wave upon wave of banner-bearing militants. Unlike those young people, the editorial board was not captivated by the presence of La Presidenta. The tone adopted was very harsh, criticizing both the current government and the candidate chosen as successor. One supposed case of misused funds was held up as a case study. At the time of writing, the Biblioteca del Congreso employed 1558 people to oversee 13 million items, while the much larger British Library employed 1490 people to oversee 150 million. A convincing counterargument initially seemed difficult to formulate. As I awaited a second *cortado*, however, a solution came to me, perfectly coherent in its logic. The number of employees could be explained were a secret second library to exist, located beneath or in invisible proximity to the first. Entertained by this possibility, I turned to the section *Espectáculos*. To my surprise I saw a tiny color-saturated photo of the man from the theater. A new work was being staged called 'Three Chimneys', the newspaper informed readers. Funds for the production came from a private personal injury settlement, and according to the reviewer the play was a success.

BAR BRITÁNICO

THE DAY A TANK drove through the plate glass window of Bar Británico, I happened to be sitting at a badly-positioned table, shoved into a corner between bar and bathroom. At the time I complained to myself about my bad luck; if the café weren't absolutely full I'd have chosen any other place. I have a very specific idea of my ideal spot: next to the window, or tucked away in some warm and welcoming corner, far from the chatter of tourists and the invisible path repeatedly traveled by the waiter. What was hardly enviable under normal circumstances, however, that day saved my life.

Those sitting beside the window died instantly. Even where I was, the damage was considerable. Shards of glass flew in our direction from seemingly unpredictable angles, or angles only predictable for someone with a solid knowledge of physics. But physics has never been my strong point; nor would it have helped in the 0.02 millisecond interval between my observation of the tank and its sudden eruption through the glass.

When I say 'tank', I want you to imagine something as concrete and solid as what confronted us. The newspapers the next day, which I wouldn't read until later, named the model: a Merkava Mark 4 equipped with a digital C4IS battle-management system, designed for maximum damage. It's not as if the loss of the bar itself were irreparable; it had never been particularly attractive, or a tourist draw like the Tortoni. It even seemed to take pride in its homely brown appearance, the poor service of its waiters, its coffee always (and this varied unpredictably) either flavorless or burnt. And yet the café had its loyal following. Lately the place had become a meeting place for gays, attracted by its discretion and lack of pretentions. A kind of neobohemia got together there frequently, filling the place with conversations amplified by wine and newspapers scattered behind.

What was I—an extremely infrequent visitor of that bar I'd never liked—doing there at all? I'll tell you now, if you can stomach a bit of metaphysics.

*

Everything you see is a replica, a live version of what already exists as descriptive information on the Internet. How can we know that what we see in reality corresponds with its virtual version? To ensure that no discrepancies exist, people have been distributed in different neighborhoods and paid to evaluate if reality matches its representation. These people are called 'confirmers'; for six months, that was my job.

The work was fairly easy. We'd be passed lists of landmarks with short descriptions, which we were requested to either confirm or alter. You might object there must be an easier way to do this. Perhaps this is the case, or perhaps not. A place like the Sacre Coeur in Paris or the Colisseum in Rome might see its image on the web corrected by anonymous users. So many people visit that real information accretes, conglomerating into an accurate representation, while misinformation drops away. But this city remains full of mysterious pockets that require state intervention in order to remain virtually up-to-date.

This is part of why I was hired. The other reason is government policy. Now that machines do everything, the constant demand is for more jobs, even if they aren't strictly required in the final account. Do the walls really need repainting? Does the street really need sweeping? Am I necessary or not? The question has never mattered much to me, then or now. Usually I was just happy to be in the open air.

But that day was particularly cold, and the pleasure of being outside has its limits. This is not an extraneous detail; if it weren't for that cold, I wouldn't have entered the café. When a growing numbness in my hands prevented me from effectively holding a pencil, I took refuge in the bar on the corner of Av. Defensa and Av. Brasil, pulling out my notebook and ordering a café doble to warm up.

Like I said, the location of the table blackened my mood, as did the sound system blaring a repetitive modern pop song. All the same, I was being productive. I'd begun to assemble a first version of my report, detailed and well-organized, with minor observational lacunae I planned to fill after finishing my coffee. That's when the tank burst in.

Scholarly books, books I will never read, give various possible explanations for the entrance of the tank. These theories can be largely divided into the following categories:

> — *The driver was lost*
> — *The driver was confused*
> — *The driver was drunk*
> — *The driver was mentally unstable*
> — *The driver had an objective, wishing to do harm to innocents out of ideology, a specific person out of revenge, or the café as a form of aesthetic protest. This category overlaps with the following*
> — *Conspiracy theories*

The reason there are so many versions is obvious. In reality, no one knows why a tank would drive at full speed through the window of that café, that day in particular. This is the fundamental and unavoidable conceptual problem.

*

At school we were always taught that machines and people possess different attributes. Yet I've never been completely able to rid myself of the feeling that the tank itself had bad intentions, that its pointer trained on the café had something malevolent in its form. Obviously this is a retrospective reconstruction of my feelings, an attempt to give them clarity. Immersed as I was in my notes, I never even saw the tank's pointer.

At the Hospital Argerich an attractive woman tended to me. The adjective 'attractive' is generally used to describe women who are well formed rather than genuinely beautiful. For this reason I would like to clarify that this one was both attractive and beautiful. Her attractiveness, however, did not appear to extend to her personality; so, at least, was my first impression. Her manner was that of distracted efficiency, bordering on irritation.

When I arrived, blood covered my hands and body, emerging from a countless number of wounds. I didn't feel much pain, likely due to shock. Some, yes; I don't wish to exaggerate. But I remained conscious, never stopped thinking. It struck me, for instance, that if the tank had crossed the Parque Lezama en route to its act of destruction, the landscape would have altered appreciably, and I'd have to redo my report. This realization increased my bitterness toward the perpetrator considerably.

*

The nurse helped me into bed and then left briefly to fetch something. My powers of attention, always operating in short bursts, now followed their natural tendency to the point of parody. The coat rack drew my attention completely: not the entire thing but a part of it, the heads of four horses, all golden. I didn't like their eyes; they didn't have eyes, just stared blindly into the room. When the nurse returned I registered that her hair wasn't gold like that of the horses, but a lovely brown. She noticed me staring fixedly. 'Do you like horses?' she asked with a new interest, while cleaning my wounds with an alcohol that made me wince. 'I don't have much experience with them,' I admitted. 'I grew up in the city.'

My own failure of invention disappointed me; so often an easy lie can smooth the way for things. Precisely at that moment, however, she'd applied the first swab soaked in ethanol, and the pain temporarily overwhelmed my creative faculties. 'I love horses,' she said to my relief. Perhaps my artless reply had nevertheless hit some target. 'I grew up in the countryside and used to have three. When I was eighteen I came here to study medicine. Now I hardly ever see animals anymore.'

'It's possible all of it has to do with that,' I murmured. 'The tension between city and country resolving itself in political violence . . .' As so often before, I'd said some non sequitur out loud I'd meant to think privately. It was alright though; she was smiling. Then she lifted her hand and applied the next swab.

*

When I opened my eyes the nurse's face was close to mine. I wasn't sure how much time had gone by. I remember starting to tell her a story, then falling asleep; it's possible this happened several times. The gray light entering the window told me it was morning; the tank incident had taken place the morning of the previous day. She pointed to a tray with orange juice, two slices of toast, a newspaper. 'Look how the papers explain it,' she said. 'According to the reports, it was a man who had a grudge against England because his father died in Malvinas.'

Could it really have been so simple? How had he got hold of the tank in the first place? But it appeared this hadn't been overly difficult. The boy had studied a few years at the military school on Avenida Almirante Brown and still had contacts there. Even if they hadn't been so crazy as to give him the tank directly, they'd entrusted him with the key, or at least left him alone with it for two minutes while they took a call. The military school was just a couple perpendicular streets from the bar; the risk of being stopped while covering that distance was small. It was early still and only a few people were out, apart from the homeless asleep on their benches.

But the most interesting questions are philosophical, not logistic. Why did this happen? What were the driver's motives? What are anyone's motives? Why do things happen the way they do?

'This is the way I see it,' said the nurse. 'The driver's girlfriend probably left him; he was desperate. He wanted to do something so grand it would transform him into myth. Of course he knew he wouldn't survive it. The choice of that set-up was necessarily ridiculous. But the extremes of death and absurdity were necessary to raise him to the level of legend; only then would she respect him.'

She finished her spiel, then blushed slightly. I looked at her without saying anything. Her version implied a deep romanticism about the act's symbolism, a symbolism taken to its extreme to negation. The entrance of the tank could stand for many things, all opposed: hatred and love, honor and self-humiliation, desire to restore good faith and death impeding this from happening.

*

My wounds healed more rapidly than expected. I took up my old job in the city again 'reconfirming' the area near the ex-Británico, and went on seeing the nurse. In the area surrounding her parents' house in the countryside, she introduced me to her horses and we explored the unmapped landscape. She wasn't far from the mark when she said the story might be sentimental, despite its macabre appearance. And not just for the driver of the tank, though who knows: perhaps her version was true. At the hospital, she only ever touched me to take temperature or change bandages, yet those were intense, hallucinogenic nights.

At some point I began to spin out a story for her, a narrative with branching possibilities regarding why the incident might have occurred. Using cliché elements (tank, honor, death, love) I produced drama and speculative entertainment, which served where clumsy attempts at conversation had not. I never knew where the tale would go next; I didn't read the newspaper to learn what 'really' happened. Everything was invented as I went along. And these stories, radiating out from a basic absurdity, laid the groundwork for an act of creation, an act whose effects would remain real even if the tank never existed at all.

LA INVISIBLA

SILENT AND WATCHFUL as always, La Invisibla moved through
the city, down avenues and past buildings. At this hour of morning the city
reduces itself to echoes and effects, unseen traces of the past: all that lingers
after the facts, when what remains are essences left behind.

Drifting silently down a street off Corrientes, she passed a restaurant where
behind a glass window, a waiter cut through the room, delivering orders to the
kitchen, preparing tables, making sure existing customers remained content.
The face of the waiter was waxy, his head slightly larger than life-size; he wore
a uniform, and though he moved delicately it would not be right to call him
delicate. When a sausage was ordered it appeared, crackling and piping hot, on
the table; a few minutes later, two freshly made empanadas joined it, along with
a bottle of wine. In going about his work the waiter followed the unseen steps of
previous *mozos*, the knowledge passed down from before.

Where was La Invisibla now? Turning to visit the Museo de Bellas Artes, where
paintings from the Novecento period were on display on the recently-opened upper
floor. All of them contained something of nightmare. In the works of Giorgio
de Chirico and Mario Sironi, people walked alone or in pairs, drifting down
abandoned streets or through empty plazas, passing palm trees framed by arches,

bronze statues, Greek marble busts. Walking across black and white tiled floors, they entered decayed villas and abandoned tenements, beneath white skies that seemed part of some other cosmos, close to but separate from the one we recognize.

These places, crafted from fantasy and dream, were colored in violently vibrant tones—magenta and blue, rust and ochre. Just outside or beyond the familiar, they might have been imaginary or existed in reality, capable of access via passage through a secret door or chance meeting with the right person. As in the children's story *The Golden Key* or the tales of Moravia, landscape was analysed as an extension of thought, and the division between mind and world disappeared absolutely.

La Invisibla passed a school, where children completed art projects on acid rain, combustion and the carbon cycle. These involved squeaky plastic sharks, bags of rice and ample quantities of Scotch tape, as well as cotton balls, cardboard cylinders and miniature palm trees. Questions were shouted about which animal eats phytoplankton (*ballena*, whale), whether the orca is a member of the dolphin family (*yes*), the structure of the respiratory system of axolotls and blob fish, unit conversion and the electromagnetic spectrum. A biology teacher reminded pupils that 'in the Atlantic tunas exist'; unseen links were sought between discrete units of knowledge, the way informational systems connect.

I felt the presence of La Invisibla brush by while sitting on a park bench with a *mate* gourd in hand, at the hour between night and day when things grew strange and uncertain. It had just rained, which amplified the effect, as after the rain everything is the same, only cleaner. Near me was a big bush with white flowers, which in the dark glowed like fire flies, and in front of it was a bird—a thrush with orange belly. With quick movements it flitted about looking for worms. Another close to it, the same species but more slender, moved in a similiar way but delicately, with quicker and lighter steps. Though they inhabited the same space, the two birds made no sign they noticed one another. Each went about its business, darting and dipping its beak into holes in the earth, occasionally resurfacing with the desired treasure.

As the minutes passed I started to discern an order in the movements, impossible though it would be to call it a pattern. The first bird came increasingly near the bush then hopped away briskly; the second approached the first before rapidly drawing away. After some time they began, slowly and indirectly, to move toward one another again. This continued for a few minutes, and despite the hesitations, recoils and uncertainties a certain progress was unmistakable. Occasionally the birds went back on their steps, returning to spaces previously inhabited or slowing to look at sky or ground, but the invisible dance never stopped.

Any interpretation I might provide would lack scientific accuracy, as not being a birdwatcher I do not know these animals' normal interactions. Did they usually take this much time to circle one another obliquely, or was this a special occasion, a build-up? Did a preordained order coordinate the movements, or were they performed purely at random, an aleatory sequence without greater meaning? I suspect the flowering bush and worms were only props or intermediaries, that the birds' primary interest was not the search for food but each other. La Invisibla, do you know what unseen impulse animates these creatures?

And how about you, reader? Do you feel La Invisibla as well? I thought I heard her whisper (her voice like the whir of traffic on the avenue I crossed leaving the park) that she feels close to all those who approach her with openness . . .

ANIMAL SPIRITS

IN THOSE DAYS all I had to my name were a certain ambition and an understanding, more or less, of how things work in this world. I lived in the tiny room of a pension on B—— street. Funds were running low; I had to think of some way to galvanize my finances, quick. That's when I decided to study animal spirits. Animal spirits are, like dark matter, a mysterious entity, insufficiently theorized yet responsible for what occurs in the universe. As space progressively disperses, it creates new physical structures at the cosmic level; analogously, there are shifts in mental architecture due to the movements of animal spirits. I am comfortable leaving the cosmos to others, yet isn't it natural that I, a humble human scientist, am interested in these enigmatic forms? An animal spirit is an impetus with tangible effects, but it cannot be isolated in a petri dish or separated out in a laboratory.

As a result I found myself sitting in a café day after day, observing a number of very interesting phenomena. One of them was the powerful economic effect of motherhood. New mothers will do anything to please their children, promote their development, advance their cerebral and spiritual progress. Animal spirits lead them to make exuberant purchases of items others would unhesitatingly leave to one side. This was an important observation; that day I had eaten only a small three-peso baguette of bread and my observational sense was highly sharpened. As a good entrepreneur and expert in animal spirits, I decided to take advantage of my investigations, promoting primitive wooden toys in the Colegiales and Belgrano R neighborhoods.

'For thousands of years mankind has existed without the Internet,' I explained to new mothers. 'Intelligence was primitive, linked to blackbirds, wild ducks and unlogged forests. Children ran free, learning to see connections between sky and earth through the organic process of trial and error. With wooden toys children will once again learn to view the world as a kind of complex assemblage, capable of fitting together in various ways.' The cheap wooden games I brought flew out of my hands, purchased for triple or quadruple their worth. A few months later I returned to the café, disguised with beard. 'Wooden games are linked to sub-development of the imagination,' I gravely informed the women. 'Video games, on the other hand, accelerate neuronal development.' Contradictory message notwithstanding, the technological products were snapped up as quickly as I could remove them from my bag. Animal spirits . . . the man who investigates them will have no problem rapidly growing rich.

How to gain access to the secrets of animal spirits? I began by asking myself the following question: What is the absolute minimum one can think? If one gives the mind absolutely nothing to feed on, none of the usual culture on which it wastes time, what is the background noise it will begin to process? Will it start to come up with original ideas, pursue ideas to surprising conclusions, reach for almost forgotten memories and anecdotes? What will happen when it is reduced to pure instinct? For some vibration will always exist, certain qualities or vestiges left when learned art and science disappear. In this sense animal spirits are the opposite of something I might call *the void*, linked in Whiteheadian terms to 'negative prehensions'—a grasped unity, a felt lack, the sensation something is missing or absence of some intangible brio.

Not all are convinced by this. A medical friend assures me that the heart is no more than a pump, and everything about it can be broken down mathematically. Hospital rounds often take the form of a question posed to oneself: 'If cardiac output is equal to mean arterial pressure divided by systemic vascular resistance, how would our management change on the basis of this measurement of pulmonary capillary wedge pressure as compared to right atrial pressure?' Similarly, he informs me that the most peaceful death possible involves terminal extubation, in which one goes into cardiac arrest and dies within minutes. The pronouncement is given following a death examination. You have to examine the pupils, ensure they're fixed and dilated, test for corneal blink reflex, check pulses, and listen for the absence of heart and lung sounds. Death is defined by a lack of breath—ah, I could go on, but it's all very mechanistic, details that miss the crux of the thing. Ladies and gentlemen, a return to first principles is elemental.

What is pertinent is that animal spirits can be manipulated. On the corner of the block where I live is a bakery called the Nueva Burdalesa. To buy a pastry there was never straightforward. First you had to take a ticket from the dispenser at the entrance; then you had to wait for your number to be called, while attempting to peer at the items on the other side of the glass through a thicket of arms and legs (the names of the little sandwiches were written in minuscule cursive font); then you'd twiddle your thumbs as your order was put through, your parcel of *medialunas* wrapped up with tape and paper by a young foreigner and slid into a bag printed with messages from the national syndicate of bakery workers; at long last you could make your way to the check-out on the other side of the room, an infinite distance at peak hours, to pay the bill and receive a printed receipt from the cashier . . .

All this is irrelevant, I know. I was distracted down this lane of thought since just this morning I passed the place, currently closed for *reformas* (not, as I heard a couple joke, *ratas*). Nor will it simply become a version of its previous self with liquor licence. Tables are being set up, new walls and ceiling constructed, floor tiles laid; in a word, the bakery now has aspirations to a café. The owner wants to create a more welcoming environment for purchases. If he were only to ask, the design ideas I might suggest . . .

The design of an interior is not the superficial practice it's made out to be; the arrangement of items, the distribution of objects in space, the sensory stimuli (sounds, scents, artworks chosen to hang on the wall) can make it one of the most complex fields in existence, affecting how humans are formed, influenced, seduced, pleased, offended, flattered, persuaded, made to feel desire . . . here there are clear applications for marketing, and all this has to do with animal spirits.

I write these notes while seated on the sidewalk in the sunshine near the Club de Pescadores in Olivos, beneath an extremely blue sky. I can hear the wind, the metallic sound of the masts of boats clanging against one another, the clamour of an approaching train . . . water splashes up against the pier, where a few men stand calmly, casting their poles into the water without speaking. Are there animal spirits about today? It does not appear that the fish are biting. I don't know much about these things, but the faces of the men when they return say everything. One of them, smart in a gray sweater and plaid shirt, winds up his cord, grips the bob with one hand and turns over the dangling hook into his upfaced palm with the other—nothing. He gets into his Renault Mégane and drives away . . . how elusive animal spirits can be . . .

ANATOMY OF A HOLD-UP

MIDNIGHT AT A BUS STOP after a gallery event, a man came up, pipe in hand. A bit too close, then he was out with it. 'Hand over everything, please,' he said, in a firm but pleasant tone. With such peaceful folk he easily achieved his objective. The norms were known, the gestures accepted. Mutual expectation required each actor to perform his role—thief or victim—then proceed on his way. Just as songs of the *patria* tend to begin with an ascending fourth, and the photographic rule-of-thirds advocates an off-center focus, so the well-executed crime possesses certain conventions. Rules are established with such clarity that they even permit certain communications within bounds. (One can always swap jokes with a traffic cop.)

Surprisingly, though, the thief didn't disappear immediately, and in those few extra seconds the long-awaited 152 arrived. 'Here it is,' he clarified, pointing at the vehicle. Only once its doors slammed shut did he vanish. If a robber goes beyond the nuts-and-bolts of monetary demand to offer helpful advice, is this a real instance of contact? Or is it simply a instinctive recourse to the set phrase, an unintentional lapse by a disoriented or inexperienced small-timer?

It is possible to dismantle the event, taking it by parts. To properly understand the anatomy of a hold-up, we must first understand the mentality of its perpetrator—the thief. Some thieves are pleasant in manner during their perpetration of a crime, others are unpleasant. Some are efficient in the amount they gather, others are not. We may therefore conclude at least four varieties of thief exist.

One can easily run through the permutations. There is the *unpleasant and efficient* thief—your garden standard who makes off with a television, what comes to mind when you think 'thief'. There is the *pleasant and efficient* thief, the tech-savvy professional with nimble gloved fingers and a detached approach that evades messy human contact. There is the *unpleasant and inefficient* thief, who so quickly finds himself out of the game—either caught red-handed and jailed, or forced into legal work or mooching after he fails to collect sufficient sums.

An illustrative example of the last. A few weeks ago I was making my way through the plaza in front of Retiro station when a couple approached. The man and woman were visibly drunk. '*Te pincho todo,*' said the man. Something pointy was pressed in my back. The day was sunny and the people lying on the hill above looked down at the scene without moving. I, on the other hand, was forced into activity. The pair pursued, quick on my heels.

Escape, exhilaration. Recuperating with a glass of wine afterward, I analyzed events. These robbers would not stay in the game for long, it was clear. Their broad daylight approach was not strategic. My money remained safely tucked away in my wallet; nothing had come of their risky play. They represented the variety of amateur thief disdained by professionals.

So much for these three categories. The enigma or 'X' in our analysis is the category that remains—*the pleasant and inefficient* thief, such as the amiable minor leaguer at the bus stop. The type of theft he perpetrates is innocuous, the sum lifted negligible. The positive impression left by his friendliness outweighs the slight distaste left by his unwilling appropriation.

Activities like his are understandable. In fact, some argue they should even be encouraged. Face-to-face transactions are increasingly rare. Supermarket conversations rarely transcend banal acquisitions of dairy and veg, and despite what film sequences may portray, waiters usually prefer to serve up food rather than chat. Robberies themselves are now mostly virtual. In a society in which freely-chosen talk so often reduces to cliché, forced or routine transactions retain the redemptive possibility of the unexpected. Pre-formulated structures like theft contain the potential for interaction and human connection.

Since the robber didn't board the bus, who knows how he spent his evening? The loot: a crumpled 20 peso note. Few restaurants remain open at that hour, and those which do offer limited options at that price. It's not unlikely he stopped at a newsstand for cigarettes or a sandwich. Did he encounter a friendly vendor there, just as disposed to transcend the mechanical phrase by avoiding it or adopting a certain tone? Or was he unlucky, confronting only the mysterious glass wall that governs most conversations?

But I'll end the dissection here, for that is an unknown only answerable by the kiosk vendor and his client—not the recent victim of a robbery, already disembarking at another stop.

PERFECTION

NO MATTER WHAT people think, cases of death by sheer terror, few and far between and questioned by science as they are, do exist. At a faculty party, a distressing incident was brought to my attention. A giraffe born in a Buenos Aires zoo, aged one year and three months, perished following her transfer to a 'private establishment' in the province. According to authorities, the creature, a female of the species *giraffa camelo pardalis*, 'entered in panic upon perceiving unaccustomed noises' her first night at new lodgings in Río Negro, and expired. Anticipating an outcry, the institution subsequently released a public statement designed to prevent legal repercussion; according to the zoo director, the giraffe, named Laura, arrived by means of a 'complex and careful operation' involving veterinarians and specialists who worked with the animal, 'first in the place of origin to accustom her to a special vehicle designed for her, then throughout the entirety of the journey itself'.

Autopsy results are being awaited to clarify the details of the death. Meanwhile, journalists have time to tease out the moral complications of the case. Laura was utterly defenseless, solo even by the casual standards of the giraffe, a species fond of an individualism of elective affinities, loose and shifting social bonds (they tend to group with others headed in the same direction); when confronted with the sounds of her unseen enemy, she reared up on her hind legs, responding with her own series of complex sounds, mews, moans, snorts, and flute-like cries, an ineffectual and particularly female response to danger (the male giraffe combats perceived threat by extending his neck and transforming it into a weapon he can pummel against opponents); upon hearing noises she grew hysterical rather than assume the ironic mode of thinking and tranquil reflection demanded by the situation (the scientific community is divided over the analytic intelligence of giraffes, physically at least so well designed by evolution, capable of reaching for acacia leaves at heights inaccessible to other animals).

The polemical element at stake in this tragedy, discussed with urgency in local news outlets, however, is not the devastating loss of animal life, but the fact Laura was in the process of being transferred to a private zoo belonging to a wealthy individual. In the eyes of certain *periodistas* carried away by their own contentious philippics, the giraffe was merely a pawn in a larger narrative involving a rich and capricious collector. It is uncomplicated to imagine the villain they have in mind: the private zoo owner who with a few phone calls to his bank can purchase four hectares of land and order the delivery of hundreds of exotic animals for his personal enjoyment. But as with most commonplaces, things are not as simple as they first appear.

The collector who has chosen to devote himself to the acquisition of objects is not necessarily the crude man driven by lucre stereotype makes him out to be. More likely he is the embodiment of modesty, the incarnation of a certain aesthetic, lacking the *amour-propre* of the artist. His idea of art is more likely to tend more toward that of the archivist, the arrangement of existing material rather than the Promethean creation of a work from scratch. Often he is marked by the desire for perfection, the obsession with perfect totality. Are we not all familiar with those English murder mysteries in which an eccentric gentleman is driven to kill in order to procure for himself an extremely rare blue butterfly specimen or medieval manuscript? The facts in this case are unclear, but it is not far-fetched to imagine that a collector ordered the giraffe to complete his set, awaiting it anxiously, and that when news reached him of its decease he was genuinely devastated, for not sentimental but philosophical reasons.

The accumulative archetype is not the only form the desire for perfection can take. At least three different models exist: the desire to complete a missing space (the desire of the collector), the desire to remedy a perceived flaw into homogeneity (the desire of the child) and the desire to maintain intact an already-existing perfection (the desire of the conservative). The collector, the child, and the conservative are marginal to the central current of society, existing as part of a world strange and apart, one tangential yet accessible to the life of the normal working adult. Their ideal of perfection is odd, amoral and occasionally impractical. Moved by aesthetic considerations, they are interested in the purely political or sentimental. Their idea of beauty frequently involves awe and belief in some reality beyond.

When I was small, a certain object in my living room fascinated me—a Persian rug. It had an intricate design made of moons, flowers and diamonds; it was perfectly symmetrical, without a single flaw. On hands and knees I studied it for hours, trying to find an error without success. Real Persian rugs always contain at least one flaw, so their perfection does not compete with the perfection of the divine. The same is true of all Islamic art: miniatures, vases, plates. There was no flaw in this one, ergo it had to be false. It was a convenient discovery, as in those days I wanted to be a hairdresser, and experimenting on my own hair was unthinkable. (Dubious forays into hair dyes would come only later.) The rug had a fringe of luminous white silk at both ends, divided into long tassels of approximately five centimeters each; many happy afternoons were spent caressing that fringe. The idea of experimenting with the tassels as if they were hair came as a revelation. I had never cut anyone's hair before, just looked at lots of pictures in magazines. But it relieved me when I deduced the rug was a fake, just in case.

With a pair of scissors I trimmed the fringe, which would retain the same form, a centimeter shorter. I went about the business with great care, gauging angles, clipping and evening. Each time I shortened one tassel, I had to level the ones beside it to keep the row straight. When I came to the last I thought I'd got it right, before noticing those from the midpoint on were shorter than those at the start. Returning to the beginning I correspondingly shortened the first ones. Trim, snip, adjust—the fringe went on shrinking. The terrible moment came at last when I saw the desired horizontal line had been achieved because there were no tassels left at all. I'd cut away every last one so only stubble remained, knots where the pattern of the rug itself began. Immediately

I feared the consequences. It would at least be preferable if the row were completely even. And so I sheared away the few tufts and knobs left until the rug gleamed nudely, hoping no one would perceive the change.

Of course the operation was noticed immediately. My mother cried when she saw what I'd done. 'Do you know how much that cost?' she said, going into my bedroom and sequestering my beloved scissors. (Most of the time I used them to cut out glossy magazine photos of famous singers, which I stuck to the walls of the room shared with my sister.) Attempting to escape punishment, I tried to convince her the Persian rug wasn't authentic. I told her it had no flaws and explained what that meant. It probably came from a factory nearby, a small suburban town in California identical to our own. She wasn't convinced. 'Whatever it was before, it's definitely flawed now,' she said, looking skeptically at the neat pile of fringe. Fluffed out, it looked like a cotton candy cloud. She took away the scissors and gave me extra dishes to wash for three weeks. After that I avoided the rug; its intricate patterns obviously carried a terrible power in their perfection, an occult power of destruction.

As one grows older one tends to incline toward a third form of perfection, which consists in wanting to keep existing beauty intact. Recently I attended a party at a local university to celebrate its anniversary. An enormous cake, ostentatious in design, was brought out to celebrate the occasion. Its perfection continued unmarred for a long stretch, which began to grow uncomfortable. No one wanted to be the first to rupture the smooth glossy surface of the icing. Its Latin motto and dark blue flag appeared aesthetically immune to human intervention. There the confection rested, perched on its stand on the freshly waxed basketball court, intact and virgin, beyond the reach of all. The same train of thought repeated in scores of different heads. Although a square of cake would undoubtedly be delicious, how could I mutilate an object of such beauty? How could I deface a thing so exquisite, disfigure such flawlessness, desecrate what is immaculate and sublime?

The situation grew unbearably tense. At last someone made the first move, a professor of history. He strode up with a determined look on his face, as if to say that after all, this was not Russia under Stalin, where the first to stop clapping during a ceremony was taken away that night by the secret police.

Approaching with his plate, which he balanced on the table, he proceeded to lift the cake slicer and plunge it in. With great decisiveness he cut two columns of sticky squares, vanilla with a layer of *dulce de leche*. The rest of us, half-heartedly distracting ourselves with gossip, stopped and looked on with astonishment. The professor was a man who usually went unnoticed, occupying himself with details of the League of Nations or the invasion of Panama. Now, in a manner entirely unprecedented, he was not the one presenting the great deeds of others but the center of attention. Feeling all eyes on him, he exaggerated his movements, pressing the blade down into the soft sponge. Ten minutes later some sense persisted of perfection surrendered, of innocence irrecuperably lost. I will admit, however, that this in no way detracted from the immense pleasure we took in the dessert.

TRANSFORMATION

IN THE MONTHS the city softened into summer, my mind did not allow me to read anything heavy. I flipped through a book of photographs called *Private diary of a nation*, showing page after page of objects and places from the past, possible clues to the country's development in the future. I looked at the 'popularísimo' Chevalier hat, the 'indispensable' anise-flavored liquor of the brand 8 Brothers, the special brand of fly spray all the rage with housewives in the city one year. I ran my finger along the outlines of figures in photos of the restaurant El Imparcial lit in neon, the cabaret Ocean Dancing on the avenue Leandro Alem, the nightclub Boîte Afrika where the author informed me that around 1974 'informal clothes for night became fashionable'. At the time 'automatic bars' and 'internal fairs' also became popular (I'm not sure I know what those things are) and the use of hair gel was suddenly ubiquitous.

In 1915 a parade of models took place at the department store Harrod's, one of the 'large shops that not only defined style for the middle class but with its system of credit made it accessible for the entire country.' An amusing newspaper article was published with the headline 'A refined pianist, unwitting passenger of Pibe Cabeza'. The names of bars (so small they are almost just counters facing the street) roll off the tongue: La peoresnada, Por si la pego, El 43, La flor del pago. I looked at Luna Park stadium before it had a roof, and at a long-haired young man, identified as 'Owe Monk, singer of the group Cons Combu, an authentic hippie'. I considered the Hindu Cinema (Lavalle 842), which only screened films featuring Brigitte Bardot. How did that country turn into this one? Or are all the apparent trends and changes only superficial illusions, in reality something else—a grand infinity into which one can at all times dip in and out, a succession of shifting presents in constant interaction with something larger?

But perhaps a structure can be discerned. At times I sensed the presence of certain connections, for instance while wandering the grid of streets in the north of the city, which all feature the names of aristocrats or military men. Here is Guillermo Rawson, the doctor-politician who established hygienic standards following the city's yellow fever epidemic and worried over the loneliness of the sick; there is Roque Sáenz Peña, the lawyer responsible for a vote both universal and secret. Figures like these, who appear in every book of national history, prompt you to draw parallels between Germany and Argentina, and between current policies and post-Versailles debt default and hyperinflation, so bad that in the interval between joining a line and reaching its front, a price might have doubled or tripled.

Comparisons like these are impossible to counteract save with pathetic rebuttals—that ultimately it is context that matters, that those times were different from these. Or that far more often, change is so gradual as to be hardly perceptible. If some small alteration were made to a newsstand, something insignificant like the ordering of publications, the color of the *kioskero*'s thermos or the lattice design of the metal rack holding magazines, it would likely go unnoticed. With the accumulation of time, however, the change would begin to assume significance, the newsstand converting into something else. A minor build-up of events or series of small adjustments in perspective can effect a fundamental alteration, constituting a change of state just like the conversion of water into ice or light fog, or the ship that had every plank replaced until it became a different ship altogether.

What is necessary is the fluctuation of an internal instability, a transformation effected after a long period of loosening. Alchemists understood that a corruption of material was necessary for change. Any object, or 'fossil', could serve as prime material. The 'accidental' was reduced to the 'essential', and these universal components could go on to become something else. An initial simplification was required to assume a different form. While alchemists wanted to produce solid items, the move now seems to be toward the ethereal. In a museum of household appliances, where all the old stoves and iron bed frames seem so tired and bulky, one wonders: Can progress be defined as the transition from heaviness to lightness? Is progress the transition from density to existence as rapid and invisible digital units?

Such considerations have begun to seem large. I note once again that the day is beautiful, that the sun is beginning to mellow and that soon it will be night. These reflections are rather exhausting, and I tell myself it would not be inappropriate to break for a glass of wine. One of the neighborhoods where one might do this, Palermo Hollywood, is a traditional stronghold of industry in the city, home to television studios, graphic design companies and other bastions of middle-class self-dubbed 'creatives'. Over the last decade the neighborhood has begun to change, losing its freshness. Brunch spots sell overpriced muffins in plazas that vend folkloric scarves to tourists; the few genuine surviving *parrillas* serve cocktails rather than cheap Malbec.

The neighborhood is a place free of history, neither *nacional & popular* nor old aristocracy but, in the way of all industry, *nouveau riche*. Remaining there too long it would be easy to grow cynical, to have one's perceptions colored until you begin to think: this city is too expensive for its cultural offerings, not worth the cost of living; it's a good time to read but not to go out; there is nothing new to see, or else the 'new' is only more of the same. In this part of the city, inertia appears to reign. And yet all the same, I know that something tangible, real and lasting is indeed taking place, and that deep change is occurring in this uneventful way, not as revolution in the street. In this place so devoid of personality, economic potential is unfolding, unfurling.

Is this the murder of a city or its rejuvenation? To consider these things at a distance, from another angle, one could do worse than look a few hundred kilometers north, since the problems of potential and transformation go beyond the borders of city, nation or even language. In one of the salons of the Casa de la Libertad hangs a painting, *The crime of Berruecos*, showing the death of Antonio Jose de Sucre, then president of Bolivia and hero of the independence movement.

Sucre was assassinated by enemies who wanted to split off part of Gran Colombia to form Ecuador, in order to oversee the new country as political leaders. In the picture Sucre's body lies in the middle of the forest; his horse flees in panic, his assassin stands with weapon drawn to the right.

Looking at the picture, initially it puzzles you, before you realize what it is you find so disturbing. At first glance there appear to be two assassins, but might these instead be distinct moments in the life of the same hired gun? There he is at two different stages: one version planning the crime, the other executing it. Yet Sucre is shown at only one moment, dead. Why didn't the painter give him the opportunity to exist prior to the event in the same way the assassin did? An amateur copy of the image, identical in all ways save for the addition of the figure of Sucre prior to his own murder, might be made.

The appended figure would walk slowly through the forest, near his own inert body but unaware of it; he would admire the flowers in the forest and the birds and stones around him while remaining oblivious to his approaching death. The thought is comforting: Although his future self approaches unceasingly, Sucre simultaneously exists as infinite potential. He will never really die but only change states, all moments of time somehow existing simultaneously. Sucre hypothetical, Sucre present—is there also a Sucre future? Can the presence of a historical figure like him also ghost the present reality outside the picture? The painting remains mute, but from the museum I can see to the plaza outside, where the Palacio del Gobierno functions in near anonymity, and men and women dance and eat chorizos with black beer.

BACK OF THE HEAD

JUST BEFORE CHRISTMAS, I walked around the streets of San Telmo looking for an interesting present. I'd already visited my favorite bookshops, and was wandering without fixed purpose. A number of interesting objects had caught my eye—a catalogue of marvelous invented creatures, a miniature statue of a greyhound—but none was quite strange enough to purchase. I was about to return home when a man across the street called my name. He'd set up an easel with large pages clipped up, in the manner of those who sell caricatures. But these faces were like none I'd seen before. Hair covered the flesh and holes on the oval where eyes and mouth should be. The heads, I realized, were in reverse.

'What's this?' I asked. I recognized him now; he was one of the bourgeois *homini novi* that roamed our streets in the new political age, lucid and entrepreneurial. And yet there was something restless and unsettled about him which I found compelling. 'I draw the back of my clients' heads instead of the front,' he explained. 'The idea is to give them a sense of the uncanny. Everyone is used to seeing their own face in the mirror and whatever is in their field of vision, which for the average human being encompasses an angle of about 70 degrees. But the back of the head holds the curious status of being a part of oneself not often thought about. Out of sight, out of mind. If you don't have one of those mirrors you can hold up to examine that part of the body, it remains invisible. Yes, imagining the back of your own head is a highly unsettling activity—try it.'

I didn't have to. I lived in an apartment with a mirror in the elevator that reflected the back of my head, not once but multiple times. It was so strange I took to looking at the ground or ceiling as I rose through the floors. Now that I had heard his spiel I began to move off; it was a warm day and a stall selling cool lime juice attracted me. But he stopped me with a strange insistence. 'Wait. Hear me out. I want you to understand.'

'When I became aware of the unsettling quality of the back of the head, I began to visit crowded public places such as football stadiums and cinemas. Soon, however, I realized it was not the phenomenon *en vivo* that interested me, but its representation. This has to do with my theory of the universe. No, don't go please! Just one minute more. History appears to be in a process of transition from the period of magic, when people were interested in mythical beasts and enchanting rites, to a purely rational reality. In the meantime the symbolic remains present, but does so in a way that is at times detached, at times hidden, at times ironic.'

'The strangeness that results from examination of the back of the head moves one to a certain reverential attitude toward all that lies beyond the visible, opening another spatial perspective that gives a clue to the unseen. The moment we become conscious it's there, we are able to reflect on another dimension of existence and access something distinct from everyday reality. Its study allows us to fill the represented world once more with gods, through the radicality of aesthetic presence transmitted through vision. The problem of the back of the head is the negative of the problem of irony, and is located at the very location where any such debate might take place (the head enclosing the mind). In this period on the threshold of pure logos, I see the examination of the back of the head as an antidote to the plague of the posturing, detached way in which moderns use their symbols.'

I wasn't sure if the man was mad or brilliant. Although I was tempted to show him the back of my own head and just leave, something retained me.

He continued: 'I knew I must not be the first one in history to realize this, so I began to systematically track the history of images of the back of the head, which appear in painting, cinema, photography, theater. The recurring image of the *cabeza en verso*, which nearly always has a startling effect, appears in the work of all cultures, and there is something beautiful about this non-specificity. People may differ in whether they choose to wear dashiki or three-piece-suits, eat pani puri or croissants. But they all share this same strange part of the body. Developing this iconology of the back of the head has occupied my time for the past three years. To make a living I dedicate myself to creating the image of the back of the head for others, as portents. There's only one problem. I've never had the courage to look at an image of the back of my own head. The very thought frightens me to an absurd degree. It's probably no more than a few wisps of hair surrounding a bald spot, yet I keep wondering—what secrets might it be hiding? What will I feel when I see it?'

I edged away slowly. He watched me go, his eyes thoughtful and melancholy. On the way toward the subway entrance I saw a table full of interesting round hats, soft, floppy and colorful, but for some reason it made me feel a little queasy to see them all piled up there in a heap.

ENCHANTED BOAT

WHENEVER WE VISITED the islands in the north of the city, things somehow seemed lighter. In the train on the way we were already floating, and by the time we arrived our feet hardly touched the ground at all. As we skipped from the squares of light in front of the cabin into shade, the tabby mirrored our steps with delicacy. Now I think it's possible she wanted to hunt us.

When the caterpillar season began on shore we amused ourselves watching them advance in small jerks. When one rippled up its nearly invisible thread from soil to roof, the analogous nature of reality became clear. Everything has its basis in pulses. A cool breeze touched the back of our necks as we looked at these things, sipping wine from long-necked glasses as long slow waves swept to shore.

We always kept the patio swept very clean. It had a plastic table and chairs where we drank coffee and read. Little rectangles of gold foil torn from champagne labels marked our pages. In the day we pulled berries from the trees, thanking our lucky stars one of us was tall enough to reach them. Other times we went swimming by the pier, and little fishes were visible just above our hands held below the water. Sometimes they startled and tried to bite. We liked to jump in but the dip was often brief, as the water was so cold and many sticks floated on the current. When we did swim it was always the same stretch following the shore's natural curve, current and countercurrent.

Afterward we'd ascend the path of stones like broken teeth to lie on a mysterious beach of white sand mixed with grass. Sprawled on towels we lifted the grains and let them fall, lifted them up and let them fall. We sprinkled them on stomach and legs, which felt so nice, then hung our towels from a branch and swung from flowering vines.

Beside this was the forest, where beasts with mirrors on their heads stamped past and incendiary plants proliferated, requiring precautionary sprinkling with anti-inflammatory dust. Lemons, lemons everywhere. Trees rustled softly, light illuminated their green. Little bits of cotton fluff drifted through the air and birds dropped in via sudden diagonals, the same way bats did at night. Overhead birds swooped by, leaving the imprint of their flight in the form of shadow.

When we got hungry we pulled up roots and plants from the earth, and put them in our baskets. Then we returned by a path made of wood planks, some missing. A black dog guided us, our cicerone. Sometimes trees fell during the storms, but with their vegetable intelligence they continued to grow: a split of the trunk sent up new life, and a movement of roots above the earth's surface retained balance.

As evening settled in, gradually saturating surroundings, we made our way back toward the ship now topped with a faint crown of smoke. A satellite and colorful cables strung low from branches once connected us to the world, but on a certain Tuesday a storm came and swept them away, and we hardly noticed the difference.

Near the water there were always many random appliances strewn about, unincorporated into the narrative of any place. Calm and silent, an old brick grill and three washing machines awaited their moment, resisting rust, new as the day they first appeared. At certain times of day we made holes in the earth, digging and digging, sticking spades in the places the soil was softest and most vulnerable. We liked to plant things instead of cutting them down.

On Christmas we looked for slender branches, twisting them into the form of a cone and tying on a gauzy blue bow. Then we went exploring until we found a bench that gave a good view of the stars. Backs pressed against wood, we looked at the moon above, gorgeous and enormous, bathed in white radiance. Constellations too, three stars close in a line, a triangle, a rhombus. Night clouds, pale in a darker sky. Coffee, pan dulce, firecrackers.

There was no way to anticipate any of this, but it pleased us very much. The world precedes human perception, and there is so much to notice.

Now I often imagine us in a boat, safe and far away from everyone. The only annoyance are the men who continue approaching in swift tiny vessels to thrust papers in our faces, attempting to seize possession of the craft. Contracts, tommy guns, steel wire. The uniforms they wear are heavy and the language they speak some incomprehensible jargon. Sign here, sign here their scribe threatens us, but wilts when informed repetition is against his own country's law. If an intruder shows up I'll give him an option: either put on a tuxedo and come eat wild peaches with us, or watch from his rowboat as we move off, tributary to open sea, skimming away along the horizon before pushing up into pale gold . . .

A USELESS OBJECT

TODAY AS USUAL, the postman came by to deliver review copies. They always come in packets, so many he often has to come by twice in an afternoon. His face is now as familiar to me as the image of our leader, but that does not imply a relationship of respect. I think he must resent the extra work; he's always shooting me suspicious glances. What he doesn't know is that I don't even want the books. So many arrive that it's impossible to keep track of them all; the nation is threatened by sinister forces and says nothing, yet goes on writing.

Last year I hired a secretary to help choose those worth attention. She had pale skin and very dark eyes; her name was Ana. In my head I secretly referred to her as Anna Snitkina, the beloved stenographer of Dostoevsky. Referred, past tense. She was a beautiful girl, but slovenly with the sorting; though I put up with it for a long time (her charms outweighed other considerations), the fact that her choices were based on wrapping rather than contents was something I could ultimately no longer ignore. Yesterday afternoon, we drank tea together, then I fired her. She left in tears; the house is now terribly quiet.

It felt good to make a firm decision after months of vacillating, but this morning I woke up doubting myself. I went to sift through the stacks of books delivered and picked up the top one at random. That's how I came across *History of a useless object*. It almost certainly would never have grabbed Ana's attention, as it was wrapped in plain brown paper with no adornments and had a cover featuring simple capitalized letters on a solid blue background. According to the back, I could expect to follow an object as it journeyed to different countries over the course of its history.

Usually I only review fiction, as this is what interests readers most. Note that I always think of the reader first, the fruit of writing criticism for a people's newspaper so many years! Yet something about this text drew me in. It had mass potential; it could be big. I took the book back to my table, its surface made of the same mass-produced wood as the chair, uncomfortable but nothing to complain about—our leader provides everything we need. There I delivered myself over to the pages.

The object in question was a glass globe, one meter in diameter, created for no purpose whatsoever. Its earliest recorded history comes from the travel diaries of a Middle Eastern merchant crossing the desert in 1428 A.D. on his way to Europe. He mentions the origins of the sphere in Africa, when sometime in the 13th century an outsider tribesman created the object, which arrived in the desert as part of the spoils of the Maghreb-Magawa war. The story is apocryphal, and difficult to believe, as it would both far precede the invention of glass and anticipate the Kantian definition of art as beauty which serves no purpose; it's more likely that the merchant, Muhammad al-Farji, created the story as a way of passing the time on camelback during the long stretches of the desert crossing.

In addition, a footnote to the text—which seems to me the key point of the book—signals that from the start the supposedly useless object was made to serve a purpose, as a truly useless object, like a truly good man, cannot exist.

Al-Farji registered that the globe was used by Mutakhar al-Rasheed, another merchant with whom he was traveling, to carry water. This was an imposition rather than a choice; the more accurate word would be punishment. Al-Rasheed was known to have a taste for liquor, but was a skilled navigator. Al-Farji, who led the exhibition, didn't want to leave him behind, but also needed to ensure he wouldn't spend his days in the howling, poetry-writing, semi-barbarian state the secret consumption of liquor produced. (No one knew where al-Rasheed obtained his spirits, or how he was able to store enough to achieve his states of intoxication; some whispered that these states were dissembled.) For the transportation of water, the only liquid permitted to the men, al-Rasheed was thus given the glass sphere, as the usual camel skin vessels could too easily be made to hide spirits. Al-Farji acquired the sphere from a local trader in exchange for nine pounds of cardamom and nine of salt.

The expedition reached Venice, where al-Rasheed disappeared. 'The globe's whereabouts during this time are unknown,' writes the author of the book; the object would not resurface until 1883, when it was catalogued as part of an antique inventory in London. It was picked up by an English lord, Sir William Mackintosh, who records his excitement over the 'glitt'ring bauble'. In the same diary, Lord Mackintosh reports contracting an unnamed Indian as his private helper and servant; this Indian would serve him for thirty years. When the lord died, his heirs fought over the rights to his property, and the Indian returned to his native country with the sphere and a few other useless items left to him in the legacy.

In the village where he was born in the south of India decades before, he had a house built with what he'd earned, which he called the Green Mansion. He was treated by those in the vicinity as a Brahmin and moneyed man, though he hadn't been either of these things when he ran away as a boy. In his notes, written in rudimentary Konkani, the Indian admitted to never having understood his eccentric master; he did not treasure the sphere left to him or see any purpose to it. Indeed, he'd forgotten about it entirely until a boy paid to help with household maintenance noticed it during the unpacking.

Rumors spread through the village like wildfire—this man, who had been gone for so long, was not just a Brahmin but a god. The glass sphere became the center of a cult. The Indian ignored the rumors at first, but his notes revealed that eventually he embraced his new status. Compared to London the village was dull; the beautiful woman he made his wife didn't speak, and was equally dull; he needed a way to entertain himself. He began to spend his days thinking up elaborate rituals and parades, in which he was carried about in a palanquin.

What happened next isn't clear, but as part of the rebellion against foreign goods and influences, he appears to have become a target. Fire was set to his mansion, but not before the globe, the notes and other objects were looted.

The glass sphere eventually made it to a local market, where a French anthropologist picked it up during his Oriental travels. It was used as part of a series of experiments on financial violence, first in the French countryside, and subsequently in the province of Buenos Aires. A nearly invisible opening in the transparent globe was made; it was stuffed with cash and handed to participants; the reactions of poor provincials attempting the impossible task of gaining access to the money were registered. The younger ones threw it on the floor or against the wall, hoping it would break; the older ones traced a finger down the side, searching for a hidden seam; the cynical of all ages did nothing, but stared at the researchers with hate in their eyes.

Word of the experiment soon got around, and the provincials held a meeting one rainy night in a tavern to discuss what to do. The entire project was an offense at every level, from the anthropological to the socioeconomic. Though at first they thought of protesting, at last it was decided the sphere should be used to their benefit. They joined leagues with a known narcotrafficker in the capital, famous for his obesity and habit of sucking olive pits; one of the anthropologists was bribed; the sphere was used to transport across provinces the cash it was convenient the bank never registered. The provincials received their cut from the transactions, which had the blessing of funding from the government, relieved foreign researchers were interested in a theme besides dictatorship. This went on for months without a hitch, but eventually one of the provincials spilled to the police; the game was up. Nothing happened to the narco, but the provincial was found dead in a field of alfalfa, and the object could clearly no longer be used. At this point, through the narco's connections, the sphere made it up to Mexico City . . .

I was taking notes as I read, but at this point I dropped my pen. With astonishment I began to read of myself, a literary critic in the D.F.; my desk was described, my lamp, the way I am sitting with head bent over my papers. The box was delivered to my house on a certain date—I checked the calendar, it is today. Here I stopped reading, suddenly frightened. How could someone know all these details, which are occurring this very minute? I need time to think through the consequences. If I keep going I might know the future; but do I want to? Instead of reading on immediately, I began to take these notes. The detail in which it has all been recorded makes me ask who could have authored such a text. It must have been someone privy to the globe's every movement, but who could that possibly be?

About a third of the book still remains; the history of the object will not end with me. Perhaps it will go to California, where it will be employed by a technological enterprise, then into space in a capsule, the emissary to alien civilizations. It might be used as the external part of a temporal telescope, which can see all segments of time and trace the movements of all objects. Is it possible this manuscript has reached me from the future? It seems improbable, yet how else could the author have known all these details—especially since the globe was never anything special, and was always a useless object? And at what point did not just the object, but a text (equally useless) *about* the sphere begin to circulate?

All this is only speculation; I haven't read beyond the present. I'm afraid to know; I've closed the book. Perhaps I will open it again, but I need to get my ideas clear first. In my city I am a literary critic of some reputation, yet I am under no illusion that I'm known beyond its borders. I have no traffic with narcos or Orientals; the question of who wrote the book, and how they know about me, intrigues and terrifies. I almost wish Ana were here so I could talk to her about this, seek her solace . . . how I regret letting her go! But maybe even she was involved? Is it mere chance the book was at the top of the pile? Perhaps she anticipated her dismissal so I could think I stumbled upon the book myself. It's possible that nothing is coincidence, that everything has been anticipated.

A knock comes at the door, a heavy pounding—once, twice, three times. I am going to go and answer . . . perhaps, as the text promises, the box with the glass sphere has arrived. If that's the case, my fingers will tremble as I pick it up; how strange it will be to have it in my hands at last, after having lived with its image over the last few hours. On the other hand, what if it isn't the sphere? What if it's somebody sent here to find me? No, better not risk it! I've long had a bag prepared for just this contingency; I'll leave by the side window now. And I'll leave these notes here just in case, so that Ana will understand if she returns.

*

The preceding pages were discovered in the apartment of J.A. Sanchez, a literary critic at one of the city's popular newspapers. His left-wing views have long been known to us; we have been following them via telephone recordings and hidden cameras for some time. The coup took place the day he was scheduled to deliver a review; he reportedly fled, leaving behind these working papers, discovered by the military forces. Two copies were made for analysis, one sent to a university in the Northeast of the United States and the other to this office in Washington.

Neither the globe mentioned nor *History of a Useless Object* has been traced. A search has begun, but we cannot rule out the possibility that Sanchez has one or both of these items on his person. Nor can we rule out the possibility that his text is pure fiction; staff psychologists report that his behavior indicates an author uninterested in continuing to serve as a mere hired pen for the government, one predisposed to wild theories and paranoid imaginative escapades.

What is clear is that Sanchez's text about *History of a Useless Object* now possesses a history of its own, existing separately from both the book that inspired it and the original sphere (whose existence, as I mentioned, is questionable). His criticism has become an object in itself, which in turn will inspire another text—this one. These histories of histories could proliferate indefinitely. I, a mediocre bureaucrat with no record of excitement in my own life, will now be joining a long historical chain, in which even the most useless objects and people play a part. My superiors will likely not approve, and the notes I send them will be suitably anodyne. But the text I am writing now will continue to circulate, with a secret life of its own . . .

INFLAMED EYE

IT WASN'T AN entirely normal day for the politician. There he was in an ophthalmologist's chair, staring at a painting of a mouth outlined in red lipstick, very white teeth inexplicably framing an eye. Something didn't seem quite right about a doctor with surrealist tastes; most medical professionals preferred dull landscapes or abstract forms, something that didn't attract the attention too much. But this one appeared to be unafraid of expressing his true preferences. Perhaps he meant to decrease the natural unease of the patient in the waiting room with a little light humor, but on him it had the opposite effect.

Casting around for something else to look at, he settled on a photo of the doctor with platinum blonde actress Mirtha Legrand, now an octogenarian at the peak of her power. The snap next to it was with Mike Tyson, who looked fresh-faced and (this was the important thing, he supposed) healthy-eyed. Had he booked an emergency visit while abroad? In any case, these photos, like the painting, had a double effect. On the one hand the celebrity patients inspired confidence. If they, with their infinite funds, chose to trust this particular doctor, wouldn't it be presumptuous for him to choose anyone else? Yet the images also seemed a touch ostentatious, the equivalent of fifteen framed degrees on the wall.

When the doctor finally called him in, he did so with a nod rather than words; during visits like these, everything was predetermined, and both already knew what to expect. The doctor opened an instructional video on a screen to explain the options. One could insert two tiny pieces of plastic in the eyelids for life (or fifteen years, which came to the same thing; the likelihood their professional relationship would last longer was beyond the realm of probability). Alternatively, one could undergo a surgery to correct vision in a more permanent way, an option that at first sight might seem expensive or drastic, but was more reasonable, the computer voice explained. Myopia was a common and easily correctable condition, and surgery was more cost-effective in the long run.

Those words, couched in the language of finance, triggered some recognition— the vocabulary of daily discussions, things read in newspapers and seen on television—though the politician wasn't sure if this recognition meant he liked the idea or not, if his continued exposure to such phrases was due to preference or circumstance. He watched the eyeball rotate on the screen, optic nerve, retina, iris, cornea, and thought of what he'd usually be doing at this time, in his office. The same rain falling outside would be outside his window as he spoke with a colleague, or more precisely, listened—he always paid a little too much attention, getting caught up in individual words, as if something like myopia of the ear existed—as he stirred a packet's worth of sugar into steaming coffee, his spoon moving in slow circles. From the eleventh floor he'd see the mud and metal of Retiro station, trains embarking on journeys to distant points of the provinces. The idea of faraway cities linked by means of efficient planning, nodes of connection that grew and strengthened with the application of scientific methods, fascinated him, and he was convinced it was the only way the nation would progress.

Then the idea came to him. Why shouldn't he do it? It would be a sort of aide memoire to remind him why he'd been attracted to his position in the first place. (He always thought of it as a 'position' and not work, a higher calling rather than an obligation, a job as old and respectable as the priesthood.) As a child he'd read stories of ancient kings who went, disguised, to examine their kingdoms. Perhaps this was a memory from his mother's Bible; he'd grown up with night-time readings and Sunday incense, and some longing for a power both sacred and true had stayed with him. This was what he wanted, not the farce of imitation glory, in halls where so often he recognized the faces of old classmates. The kingdom, after all, was not so large.

This is what he'd do then: go about the city just as in the old stories, disguised in an outfit he would never normally wear, a simple collared buttoned-up shirt and jeans, along with (why not?) a pasted-on beard. If the press found out, it'd have a field day, but it never would; anyway, it was not to be believed. Journalists reported what they suspected would happen, what was prepared in advance or what was slightly surprising but not overly so. They'd reported, for instance, on the company he'd founded with a colleague, whose proposal had been brilliant: an ecowood that didn't deform, and maintained its resistance in any climate. They'd sold it to the fathers of friends and made a fortune on country houses with requests for outer deck installation. The prices charged were high, but in the long run it was a good negotiation for the client, and everybody won. That was a possible story; this, no.

But what escaped reporting was still reality. A week later, there he was, a new man. The last touch was glasses, a tortoiseshell-rimmed pair. The mirror now reflected the face of a shabby secondary school teacher, or owner of a bookshop. He was ready. After swallowing a dram of whisky for courage, he set out to wander. The streets were marvelously open, each intersection presenting a decision that in some way resolved itself. There was a certain logic in the turnings, and though he didn't know exactly where he was, and sensed he was moving ever farther south, he couldn't say he was ever truly lost. He walked for a very long time; finally, exhausted, he sat to rest in a park under a tree with roots that looked like enormous dried-up worms from another epoch. There he carried on a chat he wasn't entirely sure how he'd begun with an elderly woman sitting on a splayed-out piece of cloth beside him.

The woman spoke of insecurity in the city in the wake of a recent crime wave, and as he listened to her ramble about the impunity of thieves, a sense of well-being pervaded him. He'd taken a few more pulls of the amber liquid on the way to sustain his energy and connect in that mystical way he was seeking with his surroundings, and though he wasn't entirely sure who'd begun the conversation, he felt he was a part of it, and it a part of him. This was what it meant to talk with the people; no poll or adviser report could replace this discourse, which took place everywhere, at the cold cut vendor's while purchasing salami and cheese, at the supermarket while picking up a packet of frozen raviolis, at the hairdresser while waiting for split ends to be snipped, but which was inaccessible to him in his role as politician. Such contact was essential. He was both a leader of the land and a citizen like the rest; he was simultaneously above the nation, part of and one with it. The body of the country was made up of nerve-like connections, fluid circulations of contacts, networks of linked cells, and his privilege lay in helping develop these combinations. He would carry the republic forward; the republic would carry him forward. The necessity for disguise was hypothetical, of course. If he were to go out in his normal state, most likely he would go unrecognized. Perhaps a few avid readers of the political pages would note his presence; at most, just as when minor theater actresses passed on the Avenida Corrientes at four in the afternoon, people would simply whisper 'Look, it's . . .' and nothing would come of it. Discreet in public, bold in private—that was the way that things worked here.

He continued to wander, had a knife fight in bar, crossed several avenues, slept a few hours by a fountain, woke without his wallet, continued on . . . it was difficult for him to remember the details now. When he got back he went directly to the bathroom and doused a washcloth with alcohol, which stung when it touched his bare skin. He had just enough presence of mind to limit his reaction to a wince rather than cry out, so as not to wake his wife sleeping in the next room. He ran himself a long hot shower to get rid of the sweat and accumulated grime of the day, then slipped into a pair of clean white pajamas and wrapped his arms around the warm body beside him. It would be impossible to hide the wound, he knew, but he'd be able to imagine a good excuse if necessary. Drifting gently to sleep, he forgot the pain, and the entire episode, welcoming oblivion.

The raw place eventually healed into a scar, the skin raised slightly in a bacillus-like shape. His prepared excuse remained tucked away like a poison pill, a reassurance for the worst that was never needed. His wife stroked the place tenderly, without ever questioning it, seemingly wanting to preserve the mystery. And that intimate gash, invisible to the public, somehow deepened the bond between them. It amplified their relationship, lent it enigmas and shadows, an insubstantiality that paradoxically became the base for greater solidity between them. He was satisfied; he had made his excursion into barbarian territory and returned safely. Now the episode was half-forgotten, and sometimes he doubted whether it had happened at all. Just like the mouth with red lipstick, however, it returned to him from time to time when least expected—a vision that was unsettling, out of place—a reminder that other worlds exist.

STORY OF A BLONDE

THERE I WAS, back in the city where I once lived. Before I got there I told myself I would only stay a while, avoiding the old haunts. I hadn't wanted to come at all; it was hard enough to get away the first time. If I returned I knew it was likely I'd never leave. But I'd been assigned to complete a white paper after touring the city's chemical factories. That was the line of work in which I found myself now; the choice was never mine.

At the factories everything seemed laughably out of date. My team was shown broken-down machines and asked if they could be reused, or in some way be made useful. Later on I attended a conference on this or that, a topic I can't remember now. At the end of the last session a colleague leaned over. 'Come along tonight, it'll be fun.' It didn't interest me, but despite myself I ended up going. My room was empty, and I was restless. At some point I lost interest though, and wandered away. The café of the petrol station across the street seemed more inviting.

It was a cold night and the sky was clear. The street was deserted, like the city had ceased to exist. But the inside of the café was full of life. Taxi drivers sat silently with cups of coffee, and there was a game of football on the television, sound turned up. I sat at a table; no one seemed to notice me. I knew the party would soon reach its peak, the collective ecstasy that hits before the rapid decline. But I didn't feel like going back in. That very energy had exhausted me, and I was happy to be where I was.

It surprised me when I saw her there, one of the circle from before. She sat in the corner eating a triangle sandwich, with a glass of beer in front. The hands that emerged from the sleeves of her blue sweater were pale. Her face was familiar, just a little more tired than I remembered. Her hair was cut short as it had been then, and was the same silver blonde. That had been her most notable feature. To style it like that had been uncommon, but what had once been daring was now conventional.

Without thinking I walked over. She looked up, startled. A flash of hatred or confusion passed over her face, or maybe that was only the way it seemed afterward. We must have exchanged some introductory words, dull phrases from a conversation book. At some point I must have commented on what she said. But in my memory she started straight in on the story, and went on talking without interruption.

*

'. . . When I left the province to come to the city, I expected an entirely different life. But somehow I found myself in a situation just like the one I'd grown up with in the suburbs. A nice house in a nice neighborhood, a furnished apartment with paintings on the walls. I had the time and resources to do what I like, so I painted a little, wrote poetry.

It pleased me to discover that his knowledge of books was so crude. A few times he tried to give his opinion on an author, convinced that what he said was correct since his teachers had said so. I felt a great tenderness, almost infinite, for him and his ignorance, a tenderness which in the end was maybe just vanity. He treated my taste for literature as something lesser, something mine. I felt happy to have my own world while he had his.

His family treated me politely while making it clear they didn't want to know anything. I liked that; I wanted to feel frivolous and strange. It became a game,

73

the difference between what others thought and our private world. From the start it was clear I would follow. The rails were in place; with him things were easy. Everything proceeded as planned, without room for disorder or chaos. Everything was controlled, even moments of abandon. The situations in which he knew what would happen in advance, and I didn't, were what we liked best. I liked to feel that anything might come to pass.

That was how it was with his appearances and disappearances. Sometimes he seemed more present when he wasn't there than when he was. He knew the effect well and measured the length of his absences, so I was nearly sick with desire when he returned, acting as if nothing was wrong. After him other men seemed annoying, overly inquisitive or too caring, as if they didn't know a little cruelty refines love, gives it unexpected edges.

When he told me what we were going to do, I remained calm. In other circumstances I would have been petrified. But I was able to maintain a steady gaze. I accepted what would happen, was even curious what it would be like. I sensed another world beyond the one I knew, more intense, more vivid, more real. I could enter that world if I agreed to what he said; what seemed strange could become pleasant, what seemed impossible probable.

The game soon escalated. But I was still able to maintain control of myself. It was going well until I learned that you would be next. It may come as a surprise, but I had kept calm until that point because I'd been thinking of you. Or not you, exactly, but that place where you had been, before. Just knowing it existed was enough for me.

You mentioned it once, do you remember? We were all at Isa's house, and you sat perched on the brown couch and described it, that protest you attended against the opening of the nuclear plant. It was enough for me to know that a place on earth still existed where this was possible, where people could do things that made events already in motion start or stop. A place where chance wasn't in control. It may seem like nothing to you, and no doubt you think I'm silly. But it's true I imagined you sitting in front of the plant cross-legged, and I returned to this image again and again. I lived in it until it came to seem more real than my own life. Of course it was impossible to remain like that forever.

My soul needed rest. Yes, I still believe in the soul, see how antiquated I am? A relic, some creature from another period or planet. Perturbing visions came to me in the day and night. I felt like I couldn't move, like time was doing strange things to loop back on itself. Without you, without the image of you, I didn't think I could go on. It got to the point that it became easier to think of doing away with my husband than you. When I realized what had happened, I came here and sat down, at this same table. I ordered a sandwich and a bottle of juice, just like now, then I stayed for a long time, waiting, as if this were enough to alter what was happening, even reverse it.'

*

The bottles glimmered on the mantel, green and yellow. The sound of a chair scraped as a taxi driver rose to leave. I got up abruptly too, and left the café. What she'd just told me should have upset me, I know. But strangely the fact that she had once planned to kill me hardly had any effect at all. What disturbed me more was what she had said about the nuclear plant. I'd never been to any protest, never sat in front of any plant. Nor did I remember ever talking about it, though there's a chance I did.

In those days sometimes I invented tales, and it was possible I had done so in that case too. Even if the events hadn't really happened, they might well have. If I'd made up a story about protesting at a nuclear plant, to create a reputation and an interesting past for myself (not for her in particular), the example I chose would have been based on a real possibility. It might as well have been true.

As for her, she was already married when I met her, one of a group that had settled down young, restoring glamour to the institution. I remembered those girls; they had been notorious. I hardly remembered her as an individual though. A face, a name; nothing more. This city makes you an amnesiac, blurring firm outlines and your sense of arrival at the present. In part that is why I finally left.

I walked around the block three or four times, too long. My limbs felt heavy in the cold. I considered returning to the party but knew I wouldn't be able to face it now. I considered going back into the café, but by this point she would probably have grown tired of waiting and left. At least I could sit down on a nearby bench and think things through.

There was her husband. He had a bottle in his hand and was on the bench where I'd been intending to sit. It didn't surprise me to see him alive. But if he wasn't dead, why had she told me that story? To lie to me the same way I had to her, as a kind of punishment? Maybe she'd found out that what I'd said wasn't true; maybe she'd wanted me to share in her terror. Was this another one of her games?

I took a step forward. I didn't know if he would even recognize me now. In the old days I had met him only once. If he attacked, would I be prepared to strike a blow? I thought I probably would, if it came to that. But he was calm, and just kept sitting. My sense of alarm dissolved; I realized my head hurt. I sat on the ground in front of him and waited for him to say something. But he didn't even register my presence.

To my surprise I realized that I was laughing. It also seemed I was lying on the pavement. I was not protesting in front of a nuclear plant, and had never done. I really should return to the party now, I thought. Or the café. But for some reason I just kept lying there. At some point I saw a figure in blue arrive. She put her arm around him, lifted him up, took him away. I remained on the ground, still laughing. This wasn't something I could stop. It went on for a long time, and then I heard footsteps. At last someone had come for me too.

LIMBO

CAT

There is a name for it. *Cognizance.* The moment you understand the nature of the world we live in. I remember exactly when it happened for me, two months after the cat appeared. When we found Morton in the closet he was a stray, mewing and hungry. With care he became fat. He had fur on his belly that reached to the ground and white paws like boots, though the rest of him was black. His eyes were green and he liked to sit on the very edge of the carpet. When his belly was rubbed he'd stretch out his paws with content, though sometimes he swiped. I loved him very much. And one day he disappeared.

Later they explained everything. My cat was dematerialized.

The world we live in is a limbo. Things exist only until they enter the 'real world'. This might happen at any moment, when they are imagined. By whom? We do not know. We are only pre-impressions. When something is created in another world, it disappears from this one. The physical laws of our land reject the existence of duplicates.

The cat in this world disappeared when the 'real' cat reached its precise age.

There must be an infinity of older felines waiting in this world as if it were a warehouse, disappearing progressively, one by one. Right now there may also exist a Jessica in the 'real world' younger than me. (If not now, someday there will be.) When she reaches my age, I will disappear.

I grieved over Morton a long time.

As days went by, the idea we are pre-impressions grew less disconcerting. Anticipation, double perception, imprints on the optic nerve that precede sight by traveling through combined brain pathways—is it really so strange premonitions such as ourselves exist? Many phenomena called 'mysterious' would be perfectly natural were one to possess more senses. There is no reason for nature to limit itself to five modes in order to match human capabilities. Experience demonstrates the reality of certain perceptions that cannot be attributed to any organ of perception.

(The adjective 'human' here is used hypothetically. We are something else.)

ATTEMPT

I made my way into the dismal village. We have them everywhere in this land. They crop up on the outskirts of forests and fields where men work, prepared to mold individual sensibilities into another form. In such villages no one is ever really happy. A man may discover his 'perfect' wife is hiding a secret, or a baby might be the pride and joy of a house until a forgotten mother comes to claim it. A girl might waste her life away caring for an ill or out-of-work partner. There is always the sense you can't quite trust your eyes. The number of hills in the distance seems to increase or decrease depending on the situation or angle. Disappearances seem more common than in other places, though probability dictates this must be an illusion.

Passing the shopfronts all the buildings seemed so thin, as if were they to be approached from another direction they'd be rendered invisible. Some people were out walking a dog, muttering to themselves at low volume. I'd heard rumors that everyone here dreamed of visiting a dismal village, as if they didn't realize just where they were. In my mind I drew up the face of the man I had to find. I began by remembering the sleeves of his shirt, then his suspenders and jacket, then finally his face, features, voice. That order was absolutely necessary in order for him to exist, even if I'd have preferred to remember him the way he looked in the picture. One hand on his waist and the other held up, like an old teapot.

There was only one bar in town, and that is where I headed. With its cushioned maroon walls and walnut paneling, its little trees at the entrance (why are there always plants in the bars of dismal villages?), its warm lighting and soft black armchairs, it would be a sensible place to while away the hours if my search yielded no results. Easily I convinced myself to enter. Bottles of scotch alternated with glasses behind the bar, and I ordered a glass of what seemed the house speciality. The television showed programs about the election, same as ever. It made you want to climb the big gold pillar connecting ceiling and floor, all the way to the screen, and change the channel to something else, anything really. Or just turn it off.

A man with a beard was reading a scientific journal and drinking beer. He seemed utterly absorbed until he turned to me. 'You look like an outsider in this town,' he said. 'Let me give you a warning. This place may generate certain emotional states. At the same time it suffers from the influences these exert. I'll put it simply. Any commonplaces can be reversed. Flesh to spirit, sentiment to intellect, sensation to thought, outsider to insider, bad taste to good, anecdote to theory, aggression to tenderness, high to low, sincerity to irony, innocence to experience.' None of this was news. I told him I had experience in this kind of place, and that there was a man I was looking for. He listened and slowly nodded. 'I suspected it,' he said. 'Follow me.' After slapping down a few notes on the counter he led me to the back of the bar, which opened onto a hallway. It looked like the mind as I used to imagine it when young, a long corridor with a series of rooms branching off. The carpet was blue and each door had gold writing.

I doubted as always, but the desire to believe got the better of me. A friend had put us in touch, then later disappeared. I tried to convince myself he was gone because he'd figured out how to escape. In the world above there would be sun, suits of rose glacé with Fontange sleeves, tuning forks, hula hoops—

of course we had these things too, somewhere, but only in potential. The day my friend gave me this contact, I passed a man in the street with the usual little jars. He stretched out his hand. 'But you do not need them. You are already happy,' he said upon seeing my face, with surprise. It was true, and that day I did believe. Later once again I began to doubt, but I came to the dismal village all the same.

The bearded man led me to a door with the surname on my slip of paper, and left. I knocked and waited. Slowly the hinge turned. Before the face of the man appeared, I could see through to the room beyond, where there was furniture, peach walls, a cat perched on the fourth shelf of a bookcase. The man had on a coat and sweater over a collared shirt.

I thought he might invite me in to sit at the table beside the window, where vines hung from ceramic pots. They must have come from far away. I was nervous as I waited for him to speak. I could think of no opening lines, nor did I wish to be the one to mention the white sky outside or some other triviality. But my fingers were crossed. How long would it take before, as always, my dreams began to seem 50-cent pieces and all my certainties became questions? The hour of repose would become the hour of chaos. I tried to focus on my hands, my legs, my feet in the same way I had imagined him before. If I could think of each part piece-by-piece and convincingly, perhaps he would leave me feeling whole.

He did not even let me in, but simply shook his head. 'All leaks in the system have been sealed,' he said. Immediately I turned to leave.

This was not my first failure.

BIRTHDAY

Birthdays are a formality because we always remain our potential age, never getting older. Time is a formality too, but it's easier to speak in terms of 'later' and 'as days went by'. If you return to the first section, you will note I used these terms when discussing my cat.

Some seek solace in religion, but this does not change the fact that they may disappear. Instead of religion, I believe in birthdays. Today I will pretend I am celebrating my 68th birthday, though really I was born in an infinite past. (Never have I *not* existed.)

I dedicate this birthday to Leopold Kronecker, the mathematician who believed in continuity rather than infinity.

Please, a toast my friends. To Morton and Leopold.

IN THE ROSE GARDEN

HE SITS AT the kitchen table, watching the curtains stamped with tiny blue flowers twisting in the wind. Outside, the silent palm trees offer no answers. The first shops are opening. The newspaper reports the upcoming agenda, Bach's concert for two violins. His thoughts are simple: sugar or not? What will he do that day? He knows himself to be a mediocre man, of solitary habits, afraid to take on the unknown. He embraced the noble profession of dentistry when, at the age of ten, he chanced upon some beautiful illustrations of mouths, showing teeth and molars, in the orthodontic advertisement of a magazine belonging to his mother. But the profession tires him. So many others in the field are not actually passionate about teeth, but simply consider them another part of the body, one that is particularly profitable. He watches the curtains, which go on twisting and twisting. The phone rings. He doesn't answer. Today he will not come in to work. Or the next day, or the day after that, or any other day at all.

What he needs, he thinks, is to embark on a completely different project. He juggles several possibilities: an investigation into olive harvesting in the north of the country; a period of travel around Europe for six years, or until he woos a rich baroness who initiates him in the delights of her labyrinthine Italian castle; a minute tracing of his genealogical tree that determines once and for all the heraldic past of his European grandfathers. But none of this inspires passion in him. Apart from dentistry, his interests are two: cigarettes and the books of the Peruvian writer Julio Ramón Ribeyro. Ultimately the mouth, the physical aspect of communication, forms the node of all his interests. Perhaps this explains his attraction to Ribeyro. The title of his collected works is *La palabra del mudo* (The Word of the Mute). The idea obsesses him in negative: the notion of those who keep their mouths shut, who can't or won't talk. In the end there's something ethical about the mouth, which can give voice to philosophical discourse, joy or misery. Triumph fills him. Yes, this is what he will do. He will embark on Ribeyro's biography, which should occupy him at least three years, working conscientiously. The stationer's at the corner sells him a block of white paper and a new ballpoint pen. He is ready to begin.

The primary problem is locating the author's collected work. Enthusiastic as he is for Ribeyro, the stories exist more vividly as memories than facts, since he left the books behind decades ago, when he moved from Lima to Buenos Aires to study. He read the stories as an adolescent at his grandmother's colonial house in Peru, where Ribeyro is a national icon. But here in Argentina his name is met with blank stares. Even in the very best shops, where the booksellers are experts on everything from *gaucho* lyrics to the correspondence of Horkheimer and Adorno, no one seems aware of Julio Ramón Ribeyro Zúñiga, winner of the Juan Rulfo prize, contemporary of Mario Vargas Llosa, one of the greatest Latin American short story writers of all time. At last, searching through library catalogues, he finds a copy of the collected works at the University of Buenos Aires's Instituto de Literatura Hispanoamericana. When he arrives on a Tuesday the library is empty, and when he asks for the book he feels his Peruvian heritage more intensely than ever.

The reading room, where he's asked to wait, makes him nervous, as does the heat. 36 degrees Celsius, no hint of ventilation. A framed photo of Ángel Rama stares down at him as he sits at the enormous table, a solid block cut from a walnut tree. On a bookshelf, three copies of the university magazine *Zama* are on display. A woman enters with a digital camera to photograph every page of a thick volume, then leaves. At last, a university employee enters and sets the book before him, disappearing without a word. He copies a few pieces of information from the prologue.

— Born 1929, died 1994
— Began studying law but dropped out, despite high marks
— Most stories set in Lima, though lived mostly in Europe
— Spent time as a hotel concierge, train station parcel carrier, newspaper collector, translator, journalist, vagabond
— The 1964 French edition of *Los gallinazos sin plumas* [Charognards sans plumes] published a photograph of a man from Mozambique, surname Ribeiro, on its author flap.

Sweltering in the heat, before reading he decides to open the doors and take in some air. On the window sill, a few plants wilt in their jars. When he unlatches the windows, an enormous dragonfly enters. He calls it a dragonfly, but it might well be some relic from a prehistoric period, when the insects were larger, with beadier eyes and wings that beat more rapidly. It alights on his trouser hem and looks at him intently. He shakes it off and moves from the window back to his chair, where his bare legs stick to the oilcloth surface. The temperature seems to be increasing, and he can't concentrate on the words dancing before him. The dragonfly flits about, landing here and there. He is the only one in the room, and the heat is suffocating. He stands up and, open to fate, decides to follow the dragonfly wherever it may lead.

The insect, after a few rapid wingbeats to the left, and then right, as if delicately considering its options, hovers in place for a minute before flitting rapidly to the next room, where the reference books are shelved. There, behind a shelf, a man consults the Alexandrine verses of André Chénier. With his drooping moustache and gait, his mixture of disillusionment and hope, he is recognisable as a character from Ribeyro's story 'The Replacement Teacher' [El profesor suplante]. The dragonfly has disappeared but it doesn't matter. Already he has decided he will follow this man wherever he might go. Tugging his moustache between two fingers as if in ecstatic understanding, the man, whose name he remembers is Matías, shuts the book and abruptly exits the room via a previously unseen staircase.

Uncapping his flask of whisky, which he keeps with him at all times to decrease his anxiety, he pursues the man via bus, taxi, bicycle and stilts—at one point they pass through a traveling circus in the Plaza Libertad—to Retiro station, where following his lead once again, he purchases a ticket and boards the Mitre train from platform four. Immediately he feels more at ease. In his literary experience, trains are places for new encounters and profound personal realizations. He settles into one of the worn red seats, framed in corroded grey metal, in the same section of four seats as the man he is following. Luckily, he seems not to notice him. A vendor passes hawking large tablets of Nestlé chocolate, wrapped in red paper. A large sign reminds them not to smoke, which makes him feel about his lapel anxiously for the familiar rectangular packet, just to know it is there. The sound of the motor begins to whir above the rails; an employee outside whistles and the train begins to move. They cast out from the station, passing huts with sheet metal roofs, orange Hamburg Sud storage boxes, murals and hanging plants, station after station. Matías gets down at Juan B. Justo, but he decides to continue to the end of the line, farther north. Why not? What does he have to lose?

Once there, he walks for a while down Avenida Maipú, then boards a bus which takes him to a station near the river. He walks a while along the shore, traipsing through mud, passing gated yacht clubs, members only. He is growing tired, but at last he finds a place of repose, a pier in an area sheltered by trees of all kinds, their trunks proudly upright. Inexplicably, it is also hedged in by roses, subtle variations on red, yellow and pink. The sky above is increasingly grey; soon it will rain. Heavy metal chains on the shore moor the boats, which sit perfectly aligned, waiting for something or perhaps simply resting. Wooden sticks float on the water and the light assumes different forms on its surface. Perhaps there are parallels with European docks, Monet's impressions. But here the fronds are larger and more threatening, the shrubs wave their spiny arms, colours and fragrances are more intense, the rustling of the trees approaches shrieking.

He sits on a bench and thumbs through the copy of *La palabra del mudo*, which he still has with him, an unintentional theft. It surprises him, as the stories in his memory have hardly anything to do with those in its pages. He recognises himself in almost every one of the characters, solitary men obsessed with compiling knowledge, with smoking, with passing the time in detailed but irrelevant observation. He extracts a Pall Mall from its packet and smokes it with relief. Ribeyro smoked too, and wrote about his obsession; in the end he died from lung cancer. His thoughts go to his tablet of white paper. He might take meticulous notes with facts like these, pages and pages of biographical information; perhaps he might find a small academic press prepared to risk publishing the biography of a foreign author. But if he does so, will that contribute to his really having lived? Above a flock of birds passes, dispersing and coming together once more. Does that mean more than a compendium of Greek symbology? Can the two things even be compared? Can any meaning be read into them?

He phones the university to apologize for his absentmindedness, promising safe delivery of the book. The voice on the other end sounds tinny, distant, unsurprised. He begins to write, the only thing he can think to do. It will be a diary composed in advance, day-by-day notes on what he will do when finally he plucks up the courage to leave his job. He knows himself to be a mediocre man, of solitary habits, afraid to take on the unknown. For now he sits at the kitchen table, watching the curtains stamped with tiny blue flowers twisting in the wind, and dreams . . .

*

INTERVIEW WITH JORGE COAGUILA

Recently I spoke with Jorge Coaguila, Lima resident and expert on Ribeyro's work. He has written and edited several books about the author, including *La palabra inmortal: conversaciones con Julio Ramón Ribeyro* (2008) and *Las respuestas del mudo: entrevistas escogidas a Julio Ramón Ribeyro* (2012).

Julio Ramón Ribeyro is repeatedly cited as one of the best contemporary short story writers in Latin America. What influence did he have on his contemporaries? Does he still exercise an influence on today's authors?

I don't think he had any influence on his contemporaries, some of whom were members of the Latin American Boom [referring to the period of the '60s and '70s when writers such as García Marquez, Vargas Llosa and Julio Cortázar came to international prominence]. In contrast, today's young authors do take him as an example, although mostly as a model of determination confronted with the difficulties of being a writer. There are also those who follow him as an example of someone who distanced himself from traditional genres by not just writing novels, poetry or theater. For example we have his diaries, his *Dichos de Luder* [in which he collected ironic sayings and short texts all attributed to a person called Luder], his 'stateless prose'.

Many of Ribeyro's stories feature a solitary figure as protagonist— an outsider, foreigner or other person who feels uncomfortable, or is seeking something that a place doesn't give him. Why was Ribeyro so interested in this theme?

Perhaps because Ribeyro himself was an outsider. In Lima he was marginalized by the well-to-do class, especially after the death of his father, which left him economically helpless. He didn't fit in with the lower classes either because of the colour of his skin. There was no room for a 'white boy' like him in the popular classes. In Europe he took odd jobs such as working as a hotel concierge, loading freight at a train station and selling old newspapers. That made him a marginal character.

I have the impression Ribeyro is fairly well known in Peru, but not necessarily outside the country. Do you agree? To what extent is that the case for Peruvian writers in general, due to the challenges of diffusion?

He isn't well-known outside of Peru, that's true. He needs greater diffusion. His books circulate very little in Spain and much less in the English-speaking or Francophone world. Ribeyro made sure his work wouldn't receive interest in other areas by not taking on exotic themes, something that attracts the European public that reads Latin American literature. He didn't set his work in the Amazon, except in one story ('Fénix'); he didn't focus on the dictators; he wasn't interested in the Andes (save for a few short stories like 'El Chaco' and the novel *Crónica de San Gabriel*).

Ribeyro spent many years in Paris, first as a student, then as a journalist for Agence France-Presse and as Peruvian ambassador. What influence did Paris and European culture have on his work?

Ribeyro spent three decades in Paris. However, he never stopped having an intense contact with Peru. That is clear from the correspondence with his older brother, Juan Antonio, with whom he exchanged views on literature, football and local politics. He often worried about his family, his mother and his siblings. His friends too. He was a great reader of French literature, a great admirer of Flaubert, Stendhal, Maupassant. He didn't know other languages besides his mother tongue and French.

What was the relationship between Ribeyro and Mario Vargas Llosa (and other Boom writers)? How did he view his own position with respect to his contemporaries?

With Cortázar he had a good friendship. With other members of the Boom, nothing except with Vargas Llosa. On that subject I have a long article, 'Story of a Friendship: Julio Ramón Ribeyro and Mario Vargas Llosa', in which I point out that the two commented on each others' work in public, above all in interviews. I also comment on the meetings they had in Paris when Vargas Llosa came to visit. Finally, I talk about their falling-out, which had to do with the support Ribeyro gave to a reform by President Alan García, a reform the liberal Vargas Llosa energetically rejected.

THE HYPERSOUND

UNDER NORMAL CIRCUMSTANCES Leo never would have visited the sauna. In a hotel there are so many other things to do; he was in a foreign land. But a kind of lassitude had overtaken him, a lack of energy. The previous night he'd suffered more than ever from back pains and acid reflux, conditions brought on by weight and stress. He looked for the hotel medic to give him some pills, but after inspecting him, the doctor gave his verdict. 'In such cases the transpiration cure is recommended. In other words, sweat it out. A flush in your cheeks will melt the distinction between yourself and world; you're too self-contained, you need that melting.' Leo's only impression of the baths came from his old bandmate, Iván. He'd been their keyboardist before he lost himself in Papua New Guinea trying to find what he called the 'hypersound', a luminous sound capable of containing contradictions, one that in some way captured or mirrored the rhythms of the universe. He constantly talked of traveling abroad to find it, then one day actually went and did it.

That had been long after the band broke up, dissolving naturally two years before when it decided to stop touring and not record another album. Back then it had been a dramatic decision, but who even remembered them now? Leo sat on a stone bench leaning against the wall and let the steam enter his pores, bringing a healthy glow to his face. Yes, he could see how this might be nice. Perhaps it was an outdated perception to think you had to be angry all the time, constantly playing the provocateur. Their band would never have survived anyway; new bands rejected the values his had maintained with pride. All of them were such nice young men and women now, youths unafraid to talk about feelings, writing surrealist lyrics offensive to no one. They'd never harbor doubts about entering a sauna like this one, never suffer his knot of complexes.

When he entered the bath, the uniformed man at the entrance informed him in a pleasant accent that it was public. Any other paying guest might also make use of it. He brushed this off; it didn't matter, who cared if some stranger saw him in the nude? He was only there a week and knew no one in the city. His record label was in full expansion, and this was supposedly the place to recruit funds and talent. And yet he couldn't help but feel self-conscious, apprehensive; his back ached, every day it was harder to get up in the morning. He was all too aware he was no longer some lithe young thing, a Greek god to gaze upon.

At least he enjoyed his current job more than his old gig as bassist. Here he was the protagonist, calling the shots. Back when the band was still together Alec always had the final word. Admittedly he'd been lead singer and guitarist; it had been his honey voice that dripped slow over the band's complex arrangements, driving girls wild. In reality it had been the arrangements that made the band great, and these had been dreamed up by Iván with his theories of the hypersound. It was an open secret Alec had never really been technically proficient at the guitar, but those squabbles didn't matter now, even if they had been key to the band's dissolution.

Leo closed his eyes and allowed the heat to slowly pervade him. Then the door opened and Alec walked in. There the two of them were, face to face, something they'd never thought would happen again.

*

After the fight, the sauna was really the only option. The city was hostile and uninteresting, and there was nowhere else to go. That morning Alec had woken and asked his girl to bring him the newspaper; she asked why, when there's a boy to do it, and when the maid came with coffee she accused him of making a pass at her. He hadn't really, at least not consciously; he just didn't think of these thin insubstantial foreigners as girls. Wasn't it a little unreasonable to complain now anyway? He must have coquetted with hundreds of *chicas* in front of her in Bogotá, many of them very forward and attractive, but somehow it was different here.

He'd met her when the band was enjoying its most hallucinatory successes. She wasn't especially beautiful or interesting, but she was always around. When, later, he began to suffer from doubt and solitude he never had to search for her, something he was particularly grateful for at those times the last thing he had the energy to do was search. When the venue cleared out following a gig—and this always happened surprisingly quickly—she continued to hang around. After a certain number of times it became a question of habit and inertia, together with, he supposed, a certain respect for her feelings.

Because she really did seem to care about him, really did seem to be there for some reason beyond his fame, which had seeped away little by little with time. So much, that although there had been a period when he resented her presence, now he was simply glad she was there—or someone, anyway; relieved he wasn't alone in this foreign hotel where he'd been asked to give a private performance to a moneyed emissary, a soulless place with him a parody of what he'd once been. He was a 'solo artist', which in practice meant a cardboard imitation of Latin rhythm who swayed his hips before amused sultans, their wives wrapped in colored cloths lounging languidly and holding oriental fans. His girl, who could seem so irritating in Bogotá, clingy and relentlessly present, was welcome in this atmosphere of anonymity.

He tried to remember why he'd gone solo in the first place. A final ceding to the temptation to bask in the full glow of fame others had deprived him of for so long. The adoration of fans all to himself without distraction, at long last. Perhaps he knew from the start it wouldn't be precisely like that, but he had to know if he could make it. To some extent, it seemed he could. But it was that 'to some extent' that bothered him most, that lack of clear success or failure. As a solo artist he'd done well, but solo artists never do *too* well.

These gigs for rich amateurs were a break to soothe his self-esteem before audiences that never demanded more than a minor spectacle. His girl had accused him of growing complacent, which had enraged him, but he had to admit she was right. Often he wondered if he should give up the game. He could manage a restaurant; he already had contacts in the city. A rock-themed dive in Buenos Aires' Palermo Hollywood wouldn't be too bad; already he could imagine the decorations, the wallpaper. A fresh start, he thought, fingers clenching his towel as the elevator descended to the hotel spa.

*

After covering the basics, to avoid speaking of themselves they spoke of others: Iván and his search for the hypersound, and the surprise when their drummer Simon took his life, although he'd seemed the most serene of them all. The conversation wound pleasantly through several tricky themes without getting bogged down in any one. After a while silence fell and they dozed a bit in the heat. Leo closed his eyes and leaned against the wall, pleasantly surprised. He felt his defenses breaking down; perhaps it wasn't so bad to have seen one another again after all; perhaps they could get along because now they were near strangers, both so different from what they'd once been.

Time passed in silence, how long was unclear. Then the uniformed man from the front desk came in, a rush of cool air entering with him; he held a tray with a note folded on it. 'For you, sir,' he said, extending it toward Alec, who took and unfolded it. His eyes scanned the paper; a deepening unease crossed his features. 'My girl,' he said simply. 'She was with me here, but now she says she's leaving . . .' 'The same one as before?' asked Leo. Alec nodded. Yet another link between them would soon disappear then. Leo hadn't really known the girl, but knew Alec would quickly meet a new one, whom he'd know even less. He tried to remember the girl's face but it escaped him. 'She's going to go visit Iván of all people. Sorry, I need to leave,' said Alec in a rush. 'I might still catch her.' 'I understand,' said Leo. He watched as Alec ran out without wiping the sweat from his face, too impatient to say goodbye before scrambling away.

He stayed a while longer, enjoying the feeling of melting into the bench and wall, thinking of nice young men and women and their modern sounds, of the strange and different ways one can lose and find oneself. Then he splashed a bucket of ice cold water over his arms and legs, wrapped himself in one of the fluffy white towels from a stack by the door, and went to go dress. He'd eat a hearty breakfast, perhaps while listening to the clear pure sound of the minarets; two hours later he'd be in a car headed to meet some fresh young musicians. He felt at peace with everything; his back and stomach no longer hurt. It didn't surprise him Alec's girl had gone to see Iván, who had always had a curious charm and was probably sitting on some beach in Papua New Guinea now, wearing a seashell headdress, sipping beer tucked into a bilum bag and conversing with his spiritual adviser as waves lapped white sand.

Everyone had always considered Iván somewhat diffuse, an impression he didn't help by relating his hazy dreams all the time and pushing the band in the direction of pools of sound, misty clouds of distortion. Leo knew better; Iván could be very concentrated and intense when he wanted, and behind all he did was an almost mathematical belief in sense and order. He'd been so upset by the contradiction of Simon's death, someone so put-together taking his own life. The hypersound had been an idea he'd picked up in a book on indigenous musicology, and though it had always inspired his compositions, after the death he'd grown obsessed with it. Contradiction reigned in everything, he said; the individual was part and parcel of the oceanic. Entering his hotel room again with a smooth swipe of his card key, Leo thought he understood. He himself was driven by lucre these days, yet it often gave him a spiritual sensation he'd never felt living in a more 'authentic' way with the band, and filled him with a strange lightness and joy.

Iván and the girl must have been writing to each other for some time, Leo supposed. Perhaps at first she'd just wanted to express her superficial problems and ask for spiritual advice, and at some point this became something else. Things would take their natural course now. Soon she'd arrive on the island, where Iván would make slow love to her. Alec would be heartbroken a while, but eventually recover enough to open the bistro he'd talked about. And though the band would never get together again, it would survive in the void of its past self, a phantasm of what it once was—the perfect embodiment of all the internal contradictions and resolutions of the hypersound.

BOUVIER

EVERYTHING HAS CHANGED now. How we think about life and death, what we notice, how we say goodbye. We see fires everywhere, a normal part of life like running water or coffee capsules or self-running lawn mowers or one-trip time travel machines or five-dimensional films, and it seems strange we could ever have existed without them, stranger still they have existed for years, taken seriously only in lore and fairy stories. Off the grid of expectations, they remained undetected by computers accustomed to analyzing big data, running semantic and quantitative analyses, creating visual renders, explaining things away with more 'likely' causes. For one can always be found; a duplicate rationale always exists. Explanatory synthesis can gloss or ignore the very thing that prances about, flickering, so tangibly calling for attention, right there.

*

I was still studying then, and in those years, the great debate carried out in journals of anthropology and at congresses concerned the value of direct experience against secondhand analysis. Bouvier, my supervisor, was firmly in the camp of those defending experience. He considered it important to be out in the field, writing as elegantly and clearly as possible, openly incorporating oneself as a first person in the description. But his critics, who advocated a computer-based approach, accused him of merely 'amassing data points'. It didn't help that he had never officially taken a doctorate, only acceding to his position on the faculty through the strength of his work, even if he was usually introduced as a 'doctor'. Bouvier's groundbreaking books had been on the role and use of amulets in New Guinea, and while some of their mystique surrounded him, his detractors spread malicious rumors that those long years in the field had also broken him.

Bouvier felt he had the logical arguments to defend himself, but to do so in this way rather than through demonstration, at a university table far from where research was carried out instead of in the field, would already communicate his defeat. He was an intelligent man and realized this, and it made him suffer a great deal. 'If they had their way, they'd take me by the wrists and force me back into my office chair . . . ,' he said, pinching his glasses between thumb and index, unsuccessfully trying to smooth down his untidy mop of hair. 'Once you've seen the things I have, it's impossible to limit oneself like that.'

The only other student Bouvier supervised was Charles. For a long time we'd been mutually aware of one another's presence, but that in itself didn't necessarily mean we'd meet. Bouvier wasn't like other professors, who held special sessions with graduate students, where a bottle of vintage wine was passed around and a more intimate setting established. He was guarded, an attitude that came either from shyness, or a vision of his profession fundamentally different from that of others. His relationship with students was individual; he insisted on meeting us separately. We were kept apart like the cells of a honeycomb.

But Charles, the idea of him, made me curious. I knew he was working on similar topics; Bouvier occasionally set books aside for him in his office, and I could get a sense of his project by reading their titles. I even knew what he looked like, since a picture of him had run once in the student book review, alongside his smooth take-down of Kluge & Malosetti. We finally crossed paths in the dining hall of my college, after the great anthology scandal. A compilation of recent anthropological work had been put together by the head of the department, a well-known figure in the field with hundreds of papers published, or so they said; I'd never looked any of them up. He'd entered the faculty relatively recently and immediately attempted to impose his methods, primarily statistical. The idea of immersion in another place he called 'antiquated', and compared it variously to literature and conceptual art. Whatever it was, it wasn't *science*. Needless to say, Bouvier was not included in his anthology.

Bouvier said nothing out loud, but a few weeks later a long and rigorously researched essay critiquing the school of thought to which the department head subscribed was published in a widely-read newspaper. A few months later a further sally was printed. The department head himself, the clear target, did not respond, but close colleagues at other institutions issued rebuttals defending his approach. This back-and-forth exchange, delayed but fatal, became a kind of venomous correspondence chess, dangerous in the extreme for Bouvier. Between him and his higher-up there now existed what amounted to open warfare.

Though my sympathies lay with Bouvier, I lacked a clear idea of how to enter the fray ideologically, as Charles had clearly done with his review piece. It was elegantly structured, like Charles himself; and now there he was in front of me, as if summoned by my thought. I'd never seen him before in my hall, where the food was tasteless but cheaper than at a café; he probably took most meals in his own hall. Later he told me he'd arranged to meet a friend from my college, an awkward young man I'd never spoken to, whose presence immediately repelled me. Known for being 'anarcho-leftist', he seemed to think much less of university studies than political agitation.

I was surprised to see them together. The impression Charles gave was of someone not particularly interested in current affairs, later confirmed when he told me he hadn't read the newspaper for years. (I now wonder whether that was really true, or just a line meant to come off as original.) Sitting next to a scruffy young man from my college whom everyone, for some reason, called the 'Louse', pale, stately Charles seemed even more attractive in contrast, leaning back slightly in his chair with an air of distraction.

That day I was alone. At the beginning of the year, as a new student, I'd felt a great deal of anxiety before every meal, and tried to find someone to accompany me. At some point doing so ceased to matter, perhaps because I'd noticed the fellows also often ate alone. I began to bring books to dinner with me. Half my attention was on Margaret Mead, the other half on the pair a few tables away, when Charles got up and walked over. I set Mead aside. 'We should meet. Charles,' he said, sticking out his hand. 'But I suppose you already know who I am.'

There was no reason to deny it. He sat down across from me and cleared up the mystery of his visit to this Hall: the Louse was editor of the book review, and they'd been discussing his next piece. I complimented the one I'd read, and talk inevitably turned to the anthology scandal. Charles voiced his full support for Bouvier; anthropology was not mathematics, he said with disdain. I listened and noted once again how clearly he stood out from the rest of the diners with his height, his almost transparent skin, his hair blond as a young boy's (usually it darkens at a certain age), his voice that was firm despite its gentleness, not at all like the grating loudness of his editor.

After returning our trays, we left Hall together, parting where the Boulevard Saint-Michel met the Rue de Vaugirard. There I turned to go back to my room; he said he would go on to a library to collect a book being held for him, but that if I liked we could meet later to continue the conversation. That night we shared a bottle of cabernet and watched a documentary series by Louis Malle about India, which had got the director banned from the country for his 'lopsided' depiction that officials said failed to respect the facts.

Charles admired Malle very much, called him brave. 'One should never be afraid to assert oneself over the surroundings,' he said. Again I noted how sure of himself he was, how much he liked to speak in declarations. At the time what struck me was his tone of confidence, the same that had suffused the review he'd written, a tone I hoped one day to acquire for myself. But now I wonder whether he said 'over' or 'in' the surroundings. Absurd to wonder about prepositions, maybe; what I really care to know is whether the seed for what he later did was already planted in his head.

*

During a supervision with Dr. Bouvier I mentioned the meeting, and his face lit up. I could see that he too was fond of him, and that this was a rare case in which he found the idea of his students making one another's acquaintance pleasing.

In the weeks that followed I went on seeing Charles, and our conversations continued. I felt he was stimulating me to think more clearly; I read as much and as deeply as I could, wanting to be more intelligent for him. Bouvier was sharp, and noticed what was going on, but never mentioned it, until one day out the blue he announced he had a project.

Although it was Charles who refined it and gave it an attractive-sounding flair, and me who smoothed the barriers that would otherwise have stood in the way of a project as ambitious as ours (considerations of cost, bureaucracy involving work with human subjects), it was Bouvier who came up with the proposal and location. He was curiously insistent on the place. Perhaps he saw his own position weakening, the head of department cutting from under his feet the pulpit of immunity he'd enjoyed for so long. Perhaps he saw it was ultimately not a battle he would likely win and chose us for his last demonstration. Whatever the case, I was flattered, and remember thinking at the time: 'Whatever happens, I will not let Bouvier down.'

We wanted to collect descriptions by peasants in the villages of Fiji of what they considered a 'just price'. Not data, but first-hand descriptions, recorded. A prestigious foundation in Paris awarded us a scholarship to further our investigations. It was a subject in vogue; few people studied tribes anymore, not only because they were going extinct, but also because they'd been rendered intellectually problematic. 'We'll write down everything they say. Or even better, we'll let them draw what they think,' speculated Charles, during the planning stages. I liked the idea, and we added it to the description on the scholarship application, copying Bouvier on our emails.

Unlike Malle, we experienced no problems with the government. In fact, it welcomed the project with open arms, even offering us various small grants; it must have seemed we were making some argument, attractive in its light heterodoxy, against a global information technology-based system that through mysterious historical circumstances had oppressed their country in particular. Later it occurred to me that the committee was likely as relieved by what the proposal wasn't interested in, as what it was. So many visiting researchers wanted to discuss the bloody political past; our project might have seemed a reprieve. Or perhaps we just all realized the violence now was primarily financial, the dollar the new dictator.

During the course of taking down responses, Charles and I continued to be with one another, in a way that was almost clinical. Not every day, but with certain regularity. From the start it had more to do with proximity and a certain intellectual affinity than real desire, or so I told myself. I had determined not to detain myself in personal questions; we were each others' instruments, using each other as was convenient and healthy.

Crossing vast stretches of empty territory we stopped at places marked off in red on a map we carried with us. I appreciated the distances; it wasn't easy to get to the last house, a clapboard wooden construction set back from the road with a long red dust path leading to its entrance and an orchard in full flower behind. Gum trees and orange plants, hibiscus and white lilies threatened to spill out from whatever unseen fence maintained them in place; the upkeep left something to be desired. On the way we'd had to ask for directions, shouting up to a tractor; a voice, no face accompanying it, explained the way. Remembering the day now, that voice seems to take on special importance. But back then its resonance didn't seem in any way eerie.

*

We were walking over the field after the last interview of the day, when we saw it. Something like pixie-light, what older travelers called a friar's lantern, and my mother when she told me stories growing up called a will-o'-the-wisp. Modern science said it was the oxidation of phosphine, diphosphane and methane, resulting in photon emissions. Yet this was something different; it gave off a blue light, an aura. A sense. I don't know how to explain it, though I'm trying my very best.

What convincing words can I use? The glow gave the idea of something alive enough to move, that came from another place. It belonged to someone, or *was* someone. Yes, for although there was no face, clearly it was him. Bouvier. The glow was silent, yet moved along playfully, as if dancing. He danced and danced, looking at us from that glow, possibly from the future or outside time itself. What was he doing there? I couldn't believe it, I cursed myself for leaving my camera in my bag in the car, I swore in disbelief. And then, just as it had come, the glow disappeared.

I looked at Charles. He was staring toward where the apparition had just been, his face white with terror, eyes wide. Did you see that, I asked. But that's impossible, he said. He's alive, in Paris. No one will believe us, it's absurd. What if impossible really means unexpected, or not yet possible, I said. No one will believe us, Charles insisted. Forget it ever happened. It never did.

This was unexpected, and I started to protest. He stared at me coldly. If you tell anyone about this, just imagine what will happen. I'll deny it. And who will they believe? You'll seem mad. You've never published a thing. I clenched my fists in frustration. He was right, of course. Who would they believe? I walked the other way, wanting to write things down, wanting to sleep alone, wanting to get away from someone who would not even entertain the possibility something might exist beyond his understanding.

Perceptual experience is what matters, I know; with big data you still only key in searches for things you expect, predetermined coordinates. But what if perceptual experience turns up something really 'unbelievable', which doesn't sync with consensus reality? Who would trust us rather than what the systemic response offered as most probable answer? Charles' eyes were cold as he maneuvered the car down that tiny country road. He would never accept a bribe, I know that. But he would deny what he saw with his own eyes to fit the data, to further his career.

Later this would be confirmed. By the time I figured out what had happened, by the time his 'forward-thinking' essays on big data technologies applied to the moral economy of Fijian peasants (*A Comparison of Individual Definitions of Just Price with Market Price*) had been published, already he was back on the continent. He'd been hired as a professor at an institute of social sciences in Stockholm, or maybe Brussels, I can't remember. I thought of fighting it, but knew no one would believe me. What does bother me is that the first thing I wanted to do in Paris was see Bouvier, and the first thing that did happen was that the message arrived.

＊

What I felt does not need to be described, though I assure you it goes far beyond anything in newspaper clippings about his passage—a peaceful yet sudden death, they say.

*

Dr Bouvier's funeral took place on a cold October day. Frost lined the great panes of the cathedral. Later I would meet some of the students he'd previously supervised. After he was lowered into the ground some of us went for beers; it was then that someone ventured to remark on the professor's constant discomfort, his agitation. Most of our group, I noted, seemed to share that nervousness. Out of coincidence, perhaps, none of us ended up staying in academia. No one except Charles. An internal review process gauging 'Quality Assurance' of Bouvier as graduate supervisor would probably dock him for his abysmal retention rate; all I know is he's the best professor I ever had.

I didn't want to spend my emotional energy on Charles. I wished him luck, kept quiet and stayed on in Paris, going on with my life. I never completed the doctorate; one day I returned my books to the library knowing I'd never read a text on indigenous islander people with such attention again. For a number of years I taught history at a secondary school—I'd become good enough at communicating during the course of my fieldwork—and then I met my husband, another teacher. I lost Charles' trace entirely, never tried to look him up.

Bouvier's image stayed with me though. One night, many years after I left academia, on a February night so cold I couldn't sleep, I dreamt of him. A vivid dream, bathed in blue. We were at his house. He told me he'd been disappointed by my decision to stop studying, which is why he hadn't visited me before now. I'd never visited him at his place before; our supervisions had always taken place at the college. It was smaller than I expected, on the outskirts of the city, lined with books from floor to ceiling and in stacks on the floor, without apparent organization.

'I've come back here to die,' he said naturally, as if this were what logic meant to him. 'But first I want to give you this.' It was an amulet from his glory days in the South Pacific. 'Of course it doesn't mean a thing,' he said, smiling slightly.

'A mere trinket. But I thought you should have it.' I accepted. He made some comments on my career, then we talked about how terrible the food in hall had been, nothing serious. When I walked to the door to leave, it was beginning to snow outside, white flakes briefly visible before dissolving imperceptibly into night. I held the brooch in my hand, a heavy thing, a deep blue sapphire embedded in gold, dangling on a chain. As I kissed Bouvier on the cheek goodbye, I looped it round my neck. Then there was only the smell of roasting coffee, my husband telling me his plans for the day, that weight on my chest.

ON THE ISLAND

NOW, WHILE THE strangeness of a certain incident is still fresh (before my memory goes completely and it's forgotten in a sort of personal historical revisionism) I'd like to document what took place during one of our trips to the Delta. When I traveled there with the writer I already knew he had made his name through disbelief in the 'work', a concept he argued was dead, to defend 'post-literary' models of the fragment and anecdote. It's no secret that at one time he had also thought of love that way, explicitly arguing there is no such thing as a 'great love', and making the claim one should live a series of intense but temporally limited relationships with realistic expectations.

I knew he was interested in the interaction between subject and object, the form in which a literary or artistic work can comment on itself or call attention to its conditions of production or industry. Likewise I knew he was interested in a relationship which did something analogous, keeping track of itself in the form of emails, diaries and public declarations. Knowing all this, and knowing he knew I knew it, the primary question was how to proceed.

Easy enough, in practice. Set aside the question, buy the tickets. The next boat departs at five o'clock.

*

We rented a house on one of the islands from a friend of his, another writer. It was the same island we'd been to twice before, accessible via a boat that departed from the main port in Tigre at regular intervals. Before handing off the key, the friend and the woman he was with showed us, step by step, how everything worked: how to operate the gas, how to filter the water from the river, how to know the tank was full when a little flag made itself visible at the top. The living room was cozy, and despite the lack of light it was easy to feel at home. Two big rugs, elegant Persian replicas, covered the floors, and a set of shelves contained a selection by Argentines and foreigners, many who had stayed there before. The books would serve as a good complement to the authors we'd brought: Goncharov, l'Isle-Adam, Papini, de Quincey.

*

The first days passed with almost unreal beauty, just like the vision of paradise in the book I was reading: slow, without sudden movements, close to nature and far from the city. It was as if time had stopped and the only objective was to love, love and be loved, love the surroundings and oneself and the person one is with, an expansive love in which the boundaries of the self dissolve and reconstitute.

We took walks along the island paths, passing the river on which sun glinted and boats floated with names only their owners could understand. Then we spread a blanket and threw ourselves on the grass behind the house. It was private there and the sun shone more strongly than it did out front. Embracing, we looked at the wavy vines, the giant and laughably useless fronds of the pumpkin plant, the rusted rectangle of propped-up metal on which mint leaves were growing.

The garden was not entirely savage. It looked as if it had been built by a previous visitor and left untended. The friend had probably grown uninterested in gardening, deliberately letting it go when he realized he'd be spending more time in the city with his partner, promoting his books. Left to their own devices the plants continued to proliferate, labyrinthine tangles almost beyond the possibility of pruning.

I rested on my back on the blanket, looking at the plants; he kept on reading. We wondered out loud about the pattern on the skin of a watermelon, the relationship between form and purpose. When the sun sunk low and a wind started up, we folded up the blanket and went inside.

*

Were the waters absolutely unruffled, is it true there was absolutely no discord whatsoever? Now, looking back, it's hard to remember. It's possible there were a few minor quarrels. It's normal for the first few days of a vacation to contain friction, though at some point things accommodate, encountering a rhythm and routine as a new home is created. My memories now, at least, are fragments of happiness. The tops of the trees swaying in the light wind. A blue sky above. A bottle of wine on the terrace. The voices of birds telling each other jokes or letting out little coos.

When we went in to drink *mate* he picked up one of the books he had brought, flipping idly through the pages without intention, just as he'd advised me to do the previous night when telling me how to catch sight of a bat at dusk: 'Look at everything but nothing in particular.' Perhaps he was waiting for some phrase to catch his eye, one we could discuss.

A brown negative fell out of the book, a photo of him taken years ago, wearing the same blue sweater he still wears. The trees behind him were the same ones as on this island. Yes, it was obvious he'd been here. He picked up the photo and looked with surprise. 'It must be strange to see a picture of yourself in which you look absolutely identical,' I said. 'Yes,' he said. 'Thirteen years ago.' 'That's a long time. But you look the same.' He nodded. 'It almost makes you begin to doubt certain things.' 'Like what?' 'I don't know. The passage of time,' he shrugged. Then he laughed and tucked the picture into his pocket. He didn't tell me anything else about it, where on the islands it had been taken, by whom. I tried to forget the image and nearly succeeded. He took my hand, and for a while it entirely left my mind.

*

Just as we'd feared when examining tiny pictures of gray rain clouds in online forecasts before leaving, the good weather didn't last. The tops of the willows began to move with a certain agitation, the sky turned white, the water started slowly but implacably to rise. I was reading under a lamp attached to the window; all at once, the text in front of me was no longer visible. The power cut affected the entire house. He considered doing nothing and waiting for the lights to return, then changed his mind and phoned the friend we'd rented from. The friend was clearly nervous about keeping the house in good condition; while showing us around he'd complained about a girl who came once and broke the control for the blinds.

'If the cut continues, you'll have no choice but to call an electrician,' he said. 'There are two: the first is expensive but knows his business, the other is my neighbor's nephew, whom you might come to an arrangement with. You can find him at the grocery. I'd recommend you stock up on provisions there too, since you might be shut in for a few days. Boots are in the cupboard in the guest bedroom, a larger and a smaller pair.' After a few more practical words he hung up.

We thought it best to take his advice, as the idea of spending several days without light, heat, water and internet was less than ideal. The house had no gas stoves, just an electric heater above the bed where we slept, in the room with the books rather than one of the other two bedrooms. We agreed that there was no point in delaying, that he'd go down to the grocery to ask about the electrician and pick up anything we needed, just in case.

*

After he left, I looked for the photo, despite myself. Perhaps it'd been snapped by someone in his past life, just like certain books he loaned me had the signature of an old lover on the upper right corner of the first page. Since it was absurd to be jealous of the past, I was not. But strange thoughts began to occur. What if past and present were somehow to fold into one, so that his younger self years ago and his present self were to overlap? What if I began to feel that he displayed a certain youthfulness and uncertainty, as if he didn't know me and wasn't comfortable yet? What if he were to forget certain details from the recent past, acting as if it were unfamiliar to the point of adopting preferences from 'before'?

Perhaps I'd suddenly grow nervous, thinking that if this were the case he might prefer a different girl—the kind he liked when he was the age in the photograph—not me, now. At that time, as he himself told me explicitly, what he looked for wasn't stability but experience. He was willing to break things off with a perfectly nice girl if that cleared the way for new sensations, new sentiments.

*

While waiting for him to return I flipped through the books on the shelf. I read an essay in the back issue of an art magazine about Marinetti's visit to Buenos Aires, a highly compact summary of the event filled with proper names that didn't offer an argument; the pieces of information seemed like unreal invisible fragments that at any moment could break off and drift away. Then I picked up a story for young boys that, although written in 1902, was still a bestseller in Russia, one which enjoyed some recognition outside the country since in 1974 Akira Kurosawa directed an adaptation.

*

Arseniev, an ethnographer exploring the taiga between China and Siberia, takes pages of careful notes: the way horses crosses the river, the best way to track down a beehive. He meets a local named Dersu, who impresses him with his goodness. Dersu always leaves a tent ready for the next anonymous traveler, an act of disinterested compassion. One night he saves Arseniev's life when during a snow storm, they are caught outside the camp site. Rather than panicking, he calmly collects grass and arranges it over them, to create a warm and dry space. Arseniev comes to think of Dersu as a friend and companion, but one night without any warning, Dersu disappears. A few months later they run into each other once again on the taiga. It does not appear that Dersu has any recollection of their time together.

*

I set the book down and tried to organize the thoughts in my mind. There was one thing I had to believe, despite whatever might appear to the contrary: that the past and present versions of a person are not totally unrelated, that although change might occur, something hard and durable remains, an essence. It was this essence I loved and not any superficial details, which were as arbitrary as proper names. It was not the blue sweater I adored, or the way he styled his hair. Some part of him remained hidden, eternal and constant, no matter the knowledge he might accrue or the theories he might discard.

It didn't matter that I had no point of comparison, that I didn't know his past self and couldn't compare it to the present. The mysterious and eternal essence in him was in some way distinguishable from accidental characteristics, even if it influenced or defined them. His self at its most fundamental seemed to me a clean metal plate on which colorful stones could be arranged in different patterns, removed and rearranged with varying degrees of skill, an infinite number of times. Considered this way, imagining him in endless variations, replicas of himself, produced in me a sensation not of anxiety but calm. This calm enabled me to proceed to further thoughts.

*

How would I know the version of him that returned would be the same as the version that left, and not, say, the version that had posed for the photo? Perhaps something in the external environment might serve as a point of comparison. But I'd never been to the house before and had no way of knowing. Nor would it be possible to judge from the grocery itself, which made a deliberate effort not to change. In appearance it could well be the same as it was thirteen years ago, only its prices showing any sign of alteration. The last time we came to this island, when we had lunch there, he said just as much.

The same purple wisteria hangs from the trellis as it did ten or twenty years ago, the same tables sell caps, beaded bracelets and scarfs with folkloric designs, the same bottles of wine and liquor are arranged on the shelf, the same man with glasses and an apron asks what you would like, the same fake blonde in full-body denim mills about preparing meals, the same brown plaid cloths cover the tables, the same old man eats an early dinner and speaks to the owner about a radio program featuring two singers (the first specializing in easy listening hits, the second in covers of Brazilians), the same never-ending game of football plays on the television, the same albums of piano music and cheerful Christmas songs alternate year-round on the disc player.

In front of the grocery is an ancient tree with roots twisted around its trunk in a knot, which might have been there from the beginning of time; a gas station on the other side of the river continues permanently unchanged; a tabby with very green eyes greets all visitors, rubbing its head against the table, waving its tail and licking its lips, the same as ever or the grown kitten of the original.

If someone really were to exist simultaneously in two moments, or to revert for some reason to a past self in a place the passage of time cannot be perceived—a place such as the grocery, the house we are renting (the friend has lived there for decades) or the islands in general—any effort at temporal location would be almost impossible, any absurd speculation justified.

*

When I saw him coming up the path with two bags in his hands, trudging through the water and mud, my heart rose and all my preoccupations fell away. Rapidly I restored the photo to its place and picked up the book about the taiga. He came in, put the bags down and took me in his arms. We embraced for a long time; then he told me what he'd brought. 'Daffodils, lots of them,' he said.

Without a word, I looked at him. That morning, we'd picked dozens of flowers from the garden and filled the rooms with them, so it was impossible even to think of buying more. He seemed to realize this too, and confusion filled his face.

'I don't know why I have these,' he said.

'Did everything go alright with the electrician?,' I asked. His face filled with even deeper confusion. 'I forgot,' he said. 'I can't believe it, but I did.' I looked at him carefully. What had happened? He'd returned and performed certain actions, which could be interpreted a number of ways. I had to choose what my reaction would be.

The decision was clear. I'd remain with him no matter what happened, even if he were to become a previous version of himself, even if time were to freeze or double back on its course. Now it was I who drew his fragile body to me. It was even amusing to imagine him as a younger version of himself. Any variation could be folded into a narrative; his self in the photo taken here and his present self shared the same essential core. He was looking at me with an odd expression, one which still hasn't gone away. But I knew then, and know now, that things will be alright.

It was simple: Even if he had reverted to a past version, one that believed in a 'series of intense but temporally limited relationships', *there was nothing to prevent these from being with the same person.* In the highly static or highly fluid time in which we exist, I can be with him in an endless number of subtly differing iterations.

Is a work more than the sum of its parts, is a person more than a series of experiences? I leave these brief notes as a first glimpse of the fragmentary being I will become, living moments of short temporal duration loosely bound by something essential and lasting, out of faith in that phrase: *I do not know what it means to have a great love, but I will love you over and over again.*

PERRINE

EVERY PERSON HAS an arbitrary origin, a place and tradition it would
be easy to inhabit. Others choose to break away and be carried along by the
unforeseen currents of life. Or is this dichotomy far too simple? In what ways
are things more complicated than this? Irrational human passions and a sense
of vocation are always tangled, in ways that seem ambiguous at the time and
afterward inevitable. Let us consider the case of Charles Dillon Perrine.

Perrine's origin was Steubenville, Ohio, a town first built to protect government
surveyors mapping the land west of the Ohio River. Later it would be referred
to as La Belle City because of its wide streets and sympathetic French influenced
architecture. Here, in a modest but comfortable apartment, Perrine was born,
the descendant of a family with earthly concerns and worldly means. One of his
ancestors was a man called The Huguenot, the founder of a Calvinist colony in
Staten Island. Another was referred to by historians as 'a merchant prince of ante-
bellum days'.

But Perrine chose to turn his eye not to earth but the heavens. He spent his
formative twenties and thirties at the Lick Observatory in California, where
he helped observe 'superluminal motion' in the nebulous clouds surrounding
the bright nova Persei, and discovered two of Jupiter's moons. He also met the

observatory librarian Bell Smith, and the two married in Philadelphia. The first few days back in California were spent in bliss, not at Perrine's home on 211 Clay Street in San Francisco, but at the nearby Hermosa Beach.

Among the photos in the observatory archives attributed to him, there is one that has nothing to do with the skies. A black dog runs down a hill, delighted by the crispness of the snow and the clear day. One imagines Perrine took the photo while walking with Bell, a momento of their love. Crystals of snow gleam in the image like stars.

Perrine traveled to Spain a few days after the wedding, taking a boat from New York. He wanted to watch an eclipse of the sun. Bell came with him, and helped develop his photos. They set up a temporary observatory and lived together. Perrine was nervous about achieving a good negative. 'I want everything to run like clockwork,' he wrote in his journal. He was able to process the film as he liked without problems, both the eclipse and other phenomena. One image of a solar eruption shows a smear of white, a mauve glow.

Perrine went on four eclipse expeditions, including to Sumatra. There he kept a diary of his travels. The journey appears to have been relaxed. 'The early morning, from daylight to nine o'clock, sees the men promenading the decks or lounging about in pajamas and loose slippers,' he wrote. 'There is no rising call or call for breakfast. One rises when he pleases (usually early, to take advantage of the coolest part of the day), bathes and breakfasts at will.' In Padang, Perrine took detailed notes on the bureaucracy, food and city. 'The streets of Padang make no more pretensions to being straight than elsewhere in the Orient, but wind about in ways most confusing to the resident of a right-angled republic,' he complained. But he concluded that 'this little-visited corner of the world offers an attractive field for the traveler who cares to go off the beaten paths.'

At the Argentine National Observatory, Perrine dedicated his time as director to counting the number of extragalactic nebulae. He also set up a huge telescope in Bosque Alegre. Thirteen comets bear his name today, discoveries or co-discoveries. He remained with Bell all his life, and never stopped visiting California. One curious work he wrote at Hermosa Beach while on vacation is called *On the Cause of the Green Ray Seen at Sunset.*

Perrine died in Villa General Mitre, a town eighty kilometers from the observatory today called Villa del Totoral. The town was once home to the Comechingone people, but now is known to visitors mostly because of the summer house rented by Rafael Alberti and Pablo Neruda. Bell stayed with him to the end. Their ending place may seem arbitrary, but is the logical consequence of anticipated and unanticipated choices made during their life journeys.

Visiting the town now, I think of Charles and Bell as I look at the paintings of Octavio Pinto, a local painter. In them, color has been applied in a deeply felt way: like love and vocation, it is simultaneously the product of chance and the result of an invisible but absolutely necessary logic. Every dab of paint lands precisely where it needs to be.

GOLDEN TRIANGLE

WHAT A BEAUTIFUL RETURN! Our car glides over empty suburban roads as we head to the golden triangle, seeking to record the birds. These are no ordinary chirps: they perfectly mimic the sound black holes make when they collide. For the last few years, the birding and physics laboratories of our university have worked together. Some on the outside claim we're mad, as deluded as those who believe they can hear the chirping of black holes without equipment. A scandal in the papers appeared when a cult group said it had progressed further in consciousness than the average human, and had special access to certain auditory frequencies. We make no such strong claims. All we say is that the sound of the birds is eerily similar to the sound of the universe, and that merit exists in analyzing it. If they'd still like to call us crazy, there's little I can do. Science is our trade, not black magic. But I'll admit that when we pinpointed where the birds lived—in the same golden triangle where I used to play, home to so many of my dearest memories—I experienced a revelatory moment. White light through pines. At that moment it did seem some arcane magic was at work.

'You are not a clever child,' they tell me. 'You are a demon. No good will come from you.' I once tricked my sister into stealing us both sherbets from the icebox when my mother wasn't looking. She was the one who got locked in her room afterward.

But a demon! Me! Really, I just like to play. Oh how I love to trick my friends, to mystify and hoodwink them . . . you can't say it's unfair, for I don't spare myself either. Yes, I also like to pull the wool over my own eyes. One thing I enjoy, to take an example, is hiding important papers, then trying as hard as possible to forget where they are. A challenge made for and by me. 'Your math homework, where is it?' my teacher asks, annoyed. I feel terrible but secretly glad, since I know I've done it and know the formulas. My intelligence is intact and grows every day. Yet the homework itself is tucked away somewhere under a couch or behind a shelf I can't recall now, nor do I have any wish to discover it.

The golden triangle is located in front of the business compound where my father used to work. We'd go there when I was young and roll down the hill, top to bottom. My sister and I raced to see who could make it first. Back then it seemed such a long way. Sometimes she won, sometimes I did. Often I wonder now if my passion for birding began in that place, where the overlapping and converging tweets of birds in the background plied subconsciously on my impressionable mind. I don't believe the mind is an empty tablet, the old materialistic idea, yet I don't think it's separate from the outside world either. Deep down I trust in the ability of the imagination to transmute sense experience into mental images, which I suspect makes me a romantic. I've spent a long time denying this, but anyone who goes into the naturalist profession is a romantic. I must admit that. Better to know yourself, yes? Even though I'm an adult now, or so they tell me, I still feel like a young woman. An imp. The activities of my team, all respected professionals, are no different from those of myself and my friends years ago, when we set out from the sandbox on adventures. Today we began our expedition at approximately eleven in the morning and now at last, at four in the afternoon, our recording devices are picking up a sound. Ch-irp! Ch-irp! It stirs us into activity. We scramble for our recording equipment. The whir of tapes begins. But where is it coming from? We search and search, but cannot detect it.

That day it was as if a little bird came up and said Follow me . . . *and whispered its secrets. I folded my voice into the landscape, tucked it away just as if it were a game. Ah! A game, played with my future self. Ch-irp! I can already see the future version of myself standing in the middle of the golden triangle (do I look pretty? am I dressed well?), looking in vain for the source of my own voice. It makes me laugh.*

A clever child. A demon child! 'Follow me,' says the bird, and shows me how to embed the sound in the landscape. I learn to make time fold over so the chirping I make will be heard years later. I'll forget the precise means by which I did this, and can't wait to forget, so it becomes a memory stored up like all the others that will emerge at random, when I smell a certain flower or eat a certain cake . . . except this one will never emerge. It will remain hidden forever, just as the universe created itself and then annihilated the memory of how it did so.

I went back to the golden triangle in my early twenties. At first I thought I'd made a mistake. It was tiny, with hardly enough room to walk about. How disappointing that the common phenomenon of things appearing smaller in real life than memory applied to me too. (What's the use of understanding something theoretically if you can't overcome it in practice?) I stood there a long moment. Then I lay down, pressed my body to the ground and hands to my chest, and tumbled down the hill just as I used to do years before. Grass stuck to my sweater and skirt and tights (thank God I had on tights!), and when I got to the bottom I lay who knows how long without moving. I must have been sad that day, or I wouldn't have visited. Though near my parents' old house, it was out of the way. Not an easy place to find unless you were trying. Perhaps I hoped to recover the simple joy I felt when younger . . . Lying there, my head pressed close to the blades of grass, I looked at the dirt and small insects. I imagined the universe mapped there too, everything a great analogy. A small ant moved up the blade, up and up and up, then sat at the top and seemed to wonder why it was there. What was it all about? Ch-irp, a bird tweeted mournfully, somewhere. That sing-song, the bird, the universe, the chirping of these words I write. The air was clear that day, the light golden. The trunks of the pines looked black against the white light. The tumble had been exhilarating, and briefly I felt happy. Eventually I knew I would have to get up, but I put it off until the mosquitoes began to bite and I got hungry. That day I had an inkling of the real nature of the universe, the perceptual relativity I'd learned about in my physics classes.

I lie pressed close to the earth, breathing. Where is the sound coming from? I must locate it. A bird swoops down from the sky and lands beside me. I half expect it to speak or sing, but it stays silent. By its fluttering of wings, I know it expects me to follow. I follow. The bird has brought the sound of the universe here, along with a different way of passing the hours and its own gravitational laws. I know if it opens its mouth, time will slow down immensely. Perhaps it will even stop, or reverse . . . The bird lands close to my face and looks at me. It is black, it remains silent. Demon! I am tired of this reality as an adult, as a scientist. Sing for me please. Sing, so I can go back to the moment of my childhood and roll down that hill. Ch-irp. 'Come on Jessi,' calls my sister. I bend my knees and crouch close to the cool earth. Then I push off, fall down the hill, tumble past and over myself into the white sky.

JESSICA SEQUEIRA writes and translates from Spanish and French.

WHAT
BOOKS
PRESS

LOS ANGELES

TITLES FROM
WHAT BOOKS PRESS

PROSE

Rebbecca Brown, *They Become Her*

François Camoin, *April, May, and So On*

A.W. DeAnnuntis, *Master Siger's Dream*

A.W. DeAnnuntis, *The Final Death of Rock and Roll and Other Stories*

A.W. DeAnnuntis, *The Mermaid at the Americana Arms Motel*

A.W. DeAnnuntis, *The Mysterious Islands and Other Stories*

Katharine Haake, *The Origin of Stars and Other Stories*

Katharine Haake, *The Time of Quarantine*

Mona Houghton, *Frottage & Even As We Speak: Two Novellas*

Rich Ives, *The Balloon Containing the Water Containing the Narrative Begins Leaking*

Annette Leddy, *Earth Still*

Rod Val Moore, *Brittle Star*

Chuck Rosenthal, *Are We Not There Yet? Travels in Nepal, North India, and Bhutan*

Chuck Rosenthal, *Coyote O'Donohughe's History of Texas*

Chuck Rosenthal, *West of Eden: A Life in 21st Century Los Angeles*

Chuck Rosenthal & Gail Wronsky, *The Shortest Farewells are the Best*

Forrest Roth, *Gary Oldman Is a Building You Must Walk Through*

Jessica Sequeira, *Rhombus and Oval*

What Books Press books may be ordered from:
SPDBOOKS.ORG | ORDERS@SPDBOOKS.ORG | (800) 869 7553 | AMAZON.COM
Visit our website at
WHATBOOKSPRESS.COM

CPSIA information can be obtained
at www.ICGtesting.com
Printed in the USA
LVOW03s0952301017

554271LV00003B/447/P